THE CALL OF THE HIGHLANDS

As their eyes met she felt herself quiver with a feeling she had never known before that seemed to be rising within her, which made her feel it was impossible to breathe.

"I may be quite wrong," the Marquess said after a moment, "but I have the feeling, Arina, that you love me."

"Yes . . . I . . . love you!" Arina whispered. "I love you . . . and I want to . . . help you . . . but I will not be a . . . nuisance and as . . . soon as you . . . want me to leave, I will do so."

"That will not be for at least a million years." As he spoke he bent forward and his lips were on hers.

She felt as if the Marquess gave her the sunshine that was outside and carried her high over the moors behind them into the sky.

The Marquess raised his head and said: "I love you . . ."

Bantam Books by Barbara Cartland
Ask your bookseller for the books you have missed

Barbara Cartland's Library of Love Series
BEYOND THE ROCKS
LOVE WEARS A VEIL

The Call of The Highlands

Barbara Cartland

BANTAM BOOKS
TORONTO · NEW YORK · LONDON · SYDNEY

THE CALL OF THE HIGHLANDS

A Bantam Book / June 1982

ISBN 0-553-22711-4

Published simultaneously in the United States and Canada

Bantam Books are published by Bantam Books, Inc. Its trademark, consisting
of the words "Bantam Books" and the portrayal of a rooster, is Registered in
U.S. Patent and Trademark Office and in other countries. Marca Registrada.
Bantam Books, Inc., 666 Fifth Avenue, New York, New York 10103.

PRINTED IN THE UNITED STATES OF AMERICA

0 9 8 7 6 5 4 3 2 1

Author's Note

"Marriage by Declaration Before Witnesses," or "Irregular Marriage," was legal in Scotland until the Act was repealed in 1949.

Until the beginning of the Eighteenth Century the Highlands stood a little apart from the rest of Scotland. The sense of isolation was engendered by feudalism, a separate language, and different forms of dress.

During the thirty-five years when not only the kilt, plaid, and pipes were banned, and of course bagpipes, the Highlanders took to carrying sticks as a substitute for the dirk. Then a shorter knife called a *skean dhu* was adopted, small enough to be concealed in a pocket or stuck in the top of a stocking.

The Celtic revival at the beginning of the Nineteenth Century was given impetus by Sir Walter Scott, and when in 1822 King George IV decided to visit his Northern Kingdom he wore the Royal Stewart tartan.

Chapter One

1803

Lord Alistair McDonon was having his breakfast.

That it was nearly noon was not surprising in the Social World in which he lived and excelled.

The night before he had been first at a dinner given by the Prince of Wales at Carlton House, then he had gone on with a number of other Bucks to the latest Dance-Hall, where the fairest and most alluring Cyprians in London paraded themselves.

As if this were not enough, he and his friends had finished up at a very expensive "House of Pleasure" in the Haymarket, where Lord Alistair now regretted that he had drunk too many glasses of French wine.

It was in fact more or less a normal evening.

At the same time, it was taking its toll the following morning, and Lord Alistair waved aside the well-cooked dish of sweetbreads and fresh mushrooms that his valet offered him and instead chose to eat toast and sip brandy.

However he was not thinking of his dry mouth or his aching head, but of the allurements of Lady Beverley.

Beside him on the table was a note, scented with an exotic fragrance, in which she informed him that she wished him to call on her at four o'clock that afternoon.

She wrote in an imperious manner which made it a command rather than a request, but that was understandable for a "Beauty" who had taken the ever-critical *Beau Monde* by storm.

The widow of a rich and distinguished land-owner in the North of England, she had come to London a year after his death, discreetly chaperoned by an elderly aunt.

Having both an impeccable reputation and a sufficiency of "blue blood," she was easily accepted by even the most strait-laced hostesses.

A new face was always an excitement in a society which had abounded in beautiful women from the time that the Prince of Wales had been captivated by the alluring actress Mrs. Robinson, and the Social World by Georgiana, Duchess of Devonshire.

Beauty had succeeded Beauty, each in the language of the St. James's Clubs "An Incomparable," and now in almost every gentleman's opinion Olive Beverley eclipsed them all.

She was certainly exquisite, with dark eyes that seemed to hold the same purple lights as those in her jet-black hair, a complexion like magnolias, and features that Lord Byron declared rivalled those of a Greek goddess.

Even the most fastidious Buck laid his heart at her feet, and although Lord Alistair disliked being one of a crowd, he finally succumbed.

Perhaps because he had been more difficult to capture than the rest, Lady Beverley had smiled on him, and finally not only was the door of her house open when he called, but so were her arms.

Despite the fact that Lord Alistair was considered a Beau and somewhat of a Dandy, he was an intelligent man.

He was well aware that his love-affair with Olive Beverley must be kept a secret, particularly from the inveterate gossips.

As the third son of a Scottish Chieftain, there was no

chance of his ever succeeding to the Dukedom, and he knew that Olive was setting her sights high.

The Duke of Torchester was squiring her to the Opera, and the Marquis of Harrowby, one of the wealthiest land-owners in England, drove her in the Park.

But there was no doubt that when they were alone she found Alistair McDonon irresistible as a lover, and their passion for each other had grown, perhaps because the very secrecy of their meetings added to the excitement.

It was unusual for Olive to send for Lord Alistair in the daytime.

As he took another sip of brandy, he read her letter again, wondering what she had to impart to him.

He had the uncomfortable feeling that it might be to tell him that Torchester or Harrowby had uttered the magic words she was wanting to hear and that she intended to be married.

If he had to lose her it would be upsetting, Lord Alistair thought, and he would certainly miss her while she was on her honeymoon.

But he thought, with a twist of cynicism at the corners of his mouth, that once the first novelty of being either a Duchess or a Marchioness was past, Olive would doubt-less once again be eager for his kisses.

"Why do I feel differently with you than with any other man?" she had asked plaintively the night before last.

He had been waiting for her in her bedroom after a dinner at Richmond House when the Marquis had escorted her home and left her at the door, where she allowed him only to kiss her hand.

Lord Alistair had entered the house in Park Street earlier through the garden door, to which he had a key.

The French window in the Drawing-Room had been left ajar, and he had slipped upstairs after the servants had gone to bed, to lie against the lace-edged pillows of her silk-draped bed.

The exotic French perfume that Olive always used scented the air, and he was quite content to wait for her, knowing that when she came they would be fired with a passion which would consume them both.

In fact, when she did arrive it was impossible for her not to fling herself into his arms, and it was a long, long time before there was any need for words. . . .

Only when the candles by the bedside were guttering low and the first soft glow of dawn was creeping up the sky were they able to talk.

"You are very beautiful!" Lord Alistair said.

He held her close against him with one arm and touched the silkiness of her dark hair with his other hand.

He had pulled the pins almost roughly from it so that it had fallen over her naked shoulders, and now he thought it was as soft as her skin, and held him captive more effectively than any chains could have done.

"What was the party like?" he asked.

"Dull!" Olive pouted. "Everybody was very grand and the Duke rather more prosy than usual."

"I am glad I was not invited."

"All I could think of," she went on, "was that I would see you later, but I never knew that time could pass so slowly! I kept looking at the clock and thinking it must have stopped!"

"Harrowby brought you home," Lord Alistair remarked. "Did he come up to scratch?"

"He would have, if I had been a little more encouraging," Olive replied complacently, "but I was afraid if he did so it would delay my being with you."

"I am flattered!"

"Why are you not more jealous?" she asked suddenly, with an angry note in her voice. "Every other man I know, including the Duke and Arthur Harrowby, would be wildly jealous and ready to shoot you dead if they knew where I was at this moment."

Lord Alistair smiled a little mockingly.

"Why should I envy anybody?"

"I love you! I love you, Alistair!" Olive said, turning her face up to his. "Do you realise you have never said that you love me?"

"I should have thought that was obvious without words," Lord Alistair replied evasively.

He knew as he spoke that Olive was disappointed because he had said no more.

But with some peculiar quirk he could not quite explain to himself, he had made it a rule never to tell any woman he loved her until he was certain that the emotion he felt for her was something very different from the burning, fiery passion for which there was another word and which was actually more descriptive.

He knew that not only in this way but in several others he was different from his contemporaries.

It had become the fashion for a gentlemen to write poetry, especially in praise of ladies they admired, and those who were unable to aspire to verse wrote eloquently and endlessly of their love.

It was now quite usual to speak of "being in love" or "making love" even to Cyprians and "bits o' muslin."

Perhaps it was because Lord Alistair had been well educated that he found it impossible to degrade the English language by using words in such a context, for they meant something very different for him.

Anyway, whatever the reason, he had never yet told any woman that he loved her, and it was inevitable that the omission should be noticed and resented.

"Tell me you love me," Olive pleaded insistently, "and tell me that when I do marry anybody else it will break your heart."

"I am not certain that I have one," Lord Alistair replied. "In fact, quite a number of lovely women have been absolutely certain that it is an organ which when I was created was omitted from my body!"

"Oh, Alistair, how can you be so cruel!" Olive cried. "You are making me think that you are playing with me, and as I love you to distraction, that is something which makes me extremely miserable!"

"I doubt it," Lord Alistair said. "But why are you worrying about words? Actions are far more effective and certainly far more satisfying."

As he spoke, his hand, which had been caressing her hair, encircled the soft pillar of her neck and his lips came down on hers.

For a moment, because she was piqued by his lack of response to her appeal, she resisted him.

Then the fierce possessiveness of his kiss awoke once again the fire within her breast, which had died down, and as the flames leapt higher and higher, matching those leaping within him, it was impossible to think but only to feel a burning, unquenchable desire.

Yesterday Lord Alistair had not seen Olive, but he had known that she was meeting both the Duke and the Marquis sometime during the afternoon and evening, and he was almost certain that she would bestow her hand on one or the other.

The strawberry leaves on a Ducal coronet were very enticing, but the Marquis was very wealthy and of the two was more attractive.

But they were both, Lord Alistair ruminated, puffed up with their own consequence.

Once Olive was the wife of either of them and was gracing the end of his table and wearing the family jewels, she would become only another possession to be prized because it was his and guarded jealously for the same reason.

It struck him that a woman's life when she married was somewhat dismal.

If her husband was important enough, she was just an adjunct to him and was not expected to have any independence in thought or feeling.

He could recall a lovely woman with whom he had had a brief but very satisfying *affaire de coeur* saying:

"The men of the *Beau Monde* are all the same! They desire you in the same way that they desire a valuable painting, a Sèvres vase, or an outstanding piece of horseflesh. But once the treasure is acquired, they are looking round for something new to add to their collection!"

"You underestimate yourself!" Lord Alistair had protested, as was expected of him.

At the same time, he knew she was more or less speaking the truth, but where he was concerned there was no collection to which a lovely woman could be added.

He had enough money to be comfortable and to meet the costs which were quite considerable for a gentleman in the most extravagant and raffish society in the whole of Europe.

He had no Estate whose rents would ensure him a large annual income, but he had no great house to keep up and therefore few expenses other than the clothes he wore, his small household in London, and the two horses which he kept for riding.

Despite this, he enjoyed a life of luxury in the houses of his friends.

Every hostess needed an unattached man, especially one as handsome and distinguished as Lord Alistair, and the invitations poured into his comfortable but comparatively modest flat in Half-Moon Street.

Because of this, he had a real need of the quiet, unassuming secretary he employed for two hours every day to answer his ever-increasing correspondence.

With his secretary to arrange his appointments, his valet to wait on him, and an experienced Chef to cook his meals when he was at home, Lord Alistair's life was one to be envied.

There was not a house in England in which he was not welcome, and the very finest hunters and steeple-chasers were at his disposal should he need them.

Perhaps more important, in all the great houses where he was entertained there was always a beautiful woman eager to see that he was not lonely during the night.

"I know you are not a rich man," the Prince of Wales had said to him a few weeks ago, "but dammit, Alistair, I believe you have a better life than I do!"

Lord Alistair had laughed.

"I think you could find a great number of men who would be only too eager to change places with you, Sire."

"Would you?" the Prince had asked pointedly.

Lord Alistair had shaken his head.

"No, Sire, but I know better than most people the many anxieties you have to bear and the difficulties you encounter in your private life."

"That is true, and I consider it extremely unfair," the Prince had exclaimed petulantly. "I envy you, Alistair—do you realise that I envy you?"

Lord Alistair had laughed about the conversation afterwards, but he had known exactly what the Prince meant.

He had thought then that he was extremely lucky in being free, unattached, and certainly not as emotionally unstable as the Prince.

In every love-affair, especially that with Mrs. Fitzherbert, he had indulged in every emotional crisis ever thought up by a playwright.

He had wept, stabbed himself with a knife, and threatened to kill himself if the recipient of his love did not respond.

Lord Alistair, who knew of his secret marriage to Mrs. Fitzherbert, thought that in fact the Prince was deranged to jeopardise his position as heir to the throne should it ever be revealed that he had married a Roman Catholic.

'No woman would ever matter so much to me,' he thought scornfully, 'that I would give up the chance of ruling Britain!'

It was the unrestrained effusions of the Prince of Wales that had made him more determined than ever not to express his feelings unless he believed with his whole heart that they were true.

Even in the greatest throes of passion, some critical faculty of his mind told Lord Alistair that this was an emotion that would eventually fade and die, and not the idealised love which he actually thought was unattainable.

And yet it had inspired great deeds, had been depicted by great artists, and had influenced composers of both music and poetry since the beginning of time.

Love! Love! Love!

Where was it to be found? And was it attainable by an ordinary man like himself?

He doubted it, and yet he refused to accept what he

knew was spurious and put it in a shrine which as far as he was concerned would remain empty.

Nevertheless, such ideals were not allowed to interfere with his enjoyment of life, and as he looked once again at Olive's scented note lying open on the table in front of him, he thought that if, as he suspected, she had chosen a husband, he would miss her.

Yet, until the day of her wedding came, he would make every effort to enjoy the time that intervened while she bought her trousseau and met her future relatives.

He was quite certain that Olive would not admit either the Duke or the Marquis to her bedroom until the ring was on her finger, while for him there was always the garden door and the unlatched window into the Drawing-Room.

Lord Alistair's reverie was interrupted by his valet coming into the Dining-Room, where the Queen Anne wall-panelling was picked out in white and gold.

It was a small room because Lord Alistair seldom entertained more than half-a-dozen friends at the same time, but, like his Sitting-Room which adjoined it, it was exquisitely decorated.

This had been a present from the very lovely lady with whom he had been enamoured nearly two years ago.

He had changed flats just as they had become lovers, and while he could afford to give her little more than flowers and trifles such as a fan or a little cameo brooch, she, because her husband was immensely rich, had expressed her feelings very generously in many different ways.

There were new horses, and very outstanding ones, in the stables which Lord Alistair rented just off Half-Moon Street.

There were also canes with gold handles, jewelled and enamelled snuff-boxes, and paintings that were undisguisedly the envy of some of Lord Alistair's friends.

If they suspected who was responsible for them, they were too tactful to say so.

They merely praised the amazing good taste and admired

the Rubens that hung over the fireplace in the Sitting-
Room and the Fragonard which graced the bedroom.

In the Dining-Room, the painting that drew the attention of those who ate there was a portrait of Lord Alistair
himself.

It had been painted when he was a boy, and in it he was
wearing the kilt, while behind him was the Castle in
which he had been born, and which he had not seen since
he was twelve.

Because it was one of the most striking and impressive
Castles in Scotland, strangers inevitably stared at the portrait but spoke of the Castle rather than of the boy who
stood in front of it.

"I have often heard of Kildonon Castle," they would
say, "and it is certainly even more impressive than I
thought any building could be."

They would want to say more, but Lord Alistair usually
changed the subject.

He was rather sensitive about the fact that he had not
been back to his native land for nearly fifteen years.

Lord Alistair's valet, Champkins, put the morning
newspaper down beside his Master and picked up the dish
of sweetbreads which he had not touched.

"A gentleman to see you, M'Lord!" he said. "I tells him
you'll see no-one this early."

"Quite right, Champkins!" Lord Alistair replied. "I have
no wish to see anybody at the moment. Tell him to come
back tomorrow."

"I tells him that, M'Lord, but he said he'd come all the
way from Scotland."

Lord Alistair looked at his valet in astonishment.

"Did you say from Scotland?" he asked.

"Yes, M'Lord, but he don't look Scottish to me, and he
speaks English like a native."

"From Scotland!" Lord Alistair said beneath his breath.
"No! That is impossible!"

"Shall I tell him to clear off, M'Lord?" Champkins asked.

There was a perceptible pause before Lord Alistair
replied:

"No, Champkins. I will see him. Ask him to come in here, and I expect he would like a drink."

"He don't look to me like the drinking sort," Champkins replied with the familiarity of a servant who has looked after his Master for a long time.

"I had better find out what he wants," Lord Alistair said. "Bring him here."

Champkins looked at his Master and Lord Alistair knew he was wondering whether to suggest that he should put on his jacket rather than wear the silk robe he had on at the moment.

He was, in fact, dressed even to his high and intricately tied white cravat, with the exception of his cut-away long-tailed coat.

If there was one thing Lord Alistair thought slovenly it was the type of gentleman who breakfasted before he had dressed and received callers with his night-shirt merely covered by a robe.

Because it was not unusual for Bucks and Beaux, including even the Prince of Wales, to drop in on friends at breakfast-time, he always washed, shaved, and dressed before he saw anybody.

The omission of his coat, which was invariably tight-fitting as the fashion demanded, was the only liberty he allowed himself at breakfast-time.

But without saying what was in his mind Champkins disappeared, and a few minutes later flung open the Dining-Room door to announce in what Lord Alistair knew was his ceremonial voice:

"Mr. Faulkner, M'Lord!"

A middle-aged man with hair grey at the temples came into the room, and for a moment Lord Alistair stared at him. Then he slowly rose to his feet and held out his hand.

"I can hardly believe that it is really Andrew Faulkner!"

"I wondered if you would recognise me, My Lord."

"I feel that is what I should be saying to you,' Lord Alistair replied.

"You have certainly grown," Mr. Faulkner remarked, "but I would have recognised you anywhere!"

His eyes rested for a moment on the painting over the mantelpiece, which was behind Lord Alistair's head, then back again to the man who clasped his hand.

"I might even say, without being impertinent, My Lord, that you look exactly as I would have expected you to, only more handsome!"

"Thank you!" Lord Alistair replied. "Sit down, Faulkner. Will you have some wine, or would you prefer coffee?"

"Coffee, if you please," Mr. Faulkner replied.

Lord Alistair nodded his head, and Champkins, who was waiting, immediately withdrew, closing the door behind him.

Mr. Faulkner sat down without hurry on a chair at the table, and Lord Alistair said:

"I presume you are here because you bring me news of my father? I cannot imagine that you have come all this way for just a friendly call."

"No, My Lord. I bring you news which I am afraid will both upset and distress you."

Lord Alistair did not speak. He merely raised his eyebrows; then, as if he felt he needed it, he drank a little more brandy.

Mr. Faulkner appeared to have difficulty in starting.

"It is, My Lord, with very great regret," he said at length, slowly and distinctly, "that I inform you that your elder brother the Marquis of Kildonon and your other brother, Lord Colin, were drowned four days ago in a storm at sea!"

Lord Alistair was as still as if he had turned to stone.

In fact, he just stared for a long time at Mr. Faulkner, as if he felt he could not have heard him a-right.

Then in a voice that did not sound like his own, he said:

"Ian and Colin are both dead?"

"Yes, My Lord."

"How could a thing like that possibly happen?"

"They were out fishing, My Lord, and a sudden storm

blew up. One can only assume that the boat was not as sea-worthy as had been believed."

"They were alone?"

"No, there was a fisherman with them, who also died."

Lord Alistair put down his brandy glass and lifted his hand to his forehead.

"I can hardly credit that what you are saying is true."

"The bodies were washed ashore, My Lord. They are being buried today in the Family Cemetery, and a great many of the Clan will be present."

Lord Alistair knew exactly what this meant. The Clansmen would come from miles over the moors as soon as the news had reached them with a summons from the Castle.

Their Pipers would come with them to join with his father's Pipers to play their laments hour after hour on the battlements.

His brothers would be lying in state in the Chief's Room, and they would be carried in procession to the Cemetery, where the Minister would read the last rites as they were lowered into the ground.

As if he waited until the picture of what was happening in Scotland had passed before Lord Alistair's eyes, Mr. Faulkner said quietly:

"His Grace, your father, My Lord, asks you to return immediately!"

Lord Alistair sat upright.

"Return? Why?"

"Because you are now, My Lord, as you must be aware, the new Marquis of Kildonon and hereditary heir to the Chieftain of the Clan."

Lord Alistair gave a little laugh that had no humour in it.

"Not a very appropriate position for somebody who has been exiled from Scotland for fifteen years."

"You are still a Scot, My Lord."

"I am aware of that, but only by blood. My life and all my interests are now very English."

"That I can understand," Mr. Faulkner said, "but your father needs you and so do the McDonons."

"They have managed very competently without me up until now."

"Because your brothers were there, they were assured of continuity when your father died."

There was just an edge on Mr. Faulkner's words, as if he thought it strange that Lord Alistair did not see the point so clearly that there was need to explain.

There was another pause before Lord Alistair asked:

"Are you telling me, Faulkner, that my father wishes me to go back and take up my life with him as if nothing has happened?"

"It is your duty, My Lord."

"Duty! Duty!" Lord Alistair scoffed. "That word covers a multitude of sins and discrepancies. If you look at it honestly, the whole thing is impossible!"

"But why, My Lord? I do not understand."

"Of course you understand, Faulkner!" Lord Alistair contradicted. "When my mother left and took me with her, she made it quite clear that she left my father with his two elder sons, but I belonged to her. I have been brought up the way she wanted and to think the way she thought."

Lord Alistair's voice was sharp as he continued:

"Because you are a friend of the family as well as my father's Comptroller, you know as well as I do that my mother's life was a living hell until she could stand it no longer."

Mr. Faulkner made a little gesture with his hands which was very explicit before he said:

"I am not pretending, My Lord, that your father and mother, while intelligent and interesting people on their own, were together anything but incompatible. But if you will forgive me saying so, even at the time I believed that your place was in Scotland, the home of your forebears, and however Anglicised you may have become, it is still Scottish blood that runs in your veins."

"Pretty words thought up by historians!" Lord Alistair sneered. "What is more important are the thoughts in my mind, the instincts of my body, and the life I have enjoyed since I have been living in the South."

"Your brothers were content."

"Because they never knew any other existence, and doubtless never had the chance of thinking for themselves as long as they were with my father."

Mr. Faulkner did not answer for a moment and Lord Alistair was sure he had scored a point that the older man found impossible to refute.

Then Mr. Faulkner said very quietly:

"There is the Clan."

"The Clan?" Lord Alistair questioned.

"What is left of them. England has neglected, oppressed, and degraded Scotland since the Duke of Cumberland won the Battle of Culloden."

"Who cares today what the Scots think or feel?"

"Perhaps only the Scots themselves," Mr. Faulkner answered, "but nevertheless they are your people, My Lord, and they look to you for leadership in the future."

"Not while they have my father ruling over them with an omnipotence that is not enjoyed by any present-day Monarch!"

"That is true," Mr. Faulkner replied. "In Scotland, especially in the North, the Chieftain is still the leader, the father, and the shepherd of his Clan."

He paused before he said gently:

"Your father is an old man, and the Clan must be assured of a successor when he dies."

"I am sure some of my many relations will be only too willing to play the part."

"Of course," Mr. Faulkner agreed unexpectedly. "Your cousin Euan, whom you will doubtless remember, after the death of your brothers offered to take your place as your father's heir and swore allegiance to him, begging him to appoint him as the next Chieftain."

There was a sudden look of anger in Lord Alistair's eyes.

"I remember Euan well!" he said. "He was always

ambitious and eager to push himself forward. What did my father say to him?"

"His Grace heard him out," Mr. Faulkner replied. "Then he said slowly and with great dignity:

" 'I have lost two sons, Euan, which is perhaps the will o' God, but I still have a third, and he is my rightful successor.' "

The way Mr. Faulkner spoke was very impressive, and there was a faint smile on Lord Alistair's lips, despite the frown on his forehead.

"I wish I could have seen my cousin's face," he remarked, "when he received the set-down he undoubtedly deserved."

"He rose to his feet," Mr. Faulkner reported, "and said:

" 'Alistair is now a Sassenach, Your Grace, and I think it unlikely he will return. If he does, you will find him a Dandy and a nincompoop, a man who is interested only in wine and women.' "

The frown deepened between Lord Alistair's eyes and his voice was hard as he asked:

"What did my father reply to that?"

"His Grace did not speak," Mr. Faulkner replied, "but merely walked from the Chief's Room, and when I followed him he told me to leave immediately for London."

There was silence and after a moment Mr. Faulkner finished:

"I came by ship because it was quicker, and I think you would find it more comfortable to travel the same way."

Lord Alistair rose to his feet.

"You are assuming that I will obey my father, but I think both you and he must realise that it is something I have no intention of doing. I may have been only twelve when I left with my mother, but she did not force me to go with her."

"I know that," Mr. Faulkner replied. "Her Grace told me that she would give you the choice."

"It was not difficult for me to make up my mind," Lord Alistair said. "I too had suffered at my father's hands. I disliked him, and I still do."

There was silence for a moment. Then Mr. Faulkner said:

"I hope it does not sound presumptuous, My Lord, when I say that whatever your feelings for him or his for you, he has been generous."

Lord Alistair stiffened, but he knew that Mr. Faulkner was speaking the truth.

When his mother had left Kildonon Castle because, as she said, it was a question of personal survival and she must either leave or die, the Duke had given her an allowance to support herself and her youngest son.

Daughter of the Earl of Harlow, she had gone home, taking Alistair with her, and had sent him first to a famous English Public School and then to Oxford.

He was brought up on the Harlow Estates in Suffolk and whenever he went to London had been able to stay at his grandfather's house in Grosvenor Square.

He had made friends and been accepted with his mother by the highest and most distinguished people in the land.

Because it all had been so new and exciting he had never for one moment missed the great Castle standing in acres of wild moorland or even his elder brothers, who had often bullied him.

When his mother had died three years ago, he had been apprehensive that he might have to change his way of living considerably if his father, who had not communicated with him in any way since he left Scotland, cut off the monies which had been paid to his wife.

It had been a great relief when he had received notice from the Duke's Attorneys that the same allowance that the Duchess had received during her lifetime would be transferred to him.

He had not written to his father personally a letter of thanks, but had asked the Attorneys to convey his gratitude.

Rather sharply, because he was perturbed, Lord Alistair asked:

"Are you saying that if I do not return, Faulkner, as my father orders, he will cut me off with the proverbial shilling?"

He knew as he waited for an answer that Mr. Faulkner was feeling for words. Then he said:

"Knowing His Grace as I do, My Lord, I think if you refuse the responsibility which your father believes is the will of God, then you will cease from that moment to be his son! He will in fact disown you!"

"And put Euan in my place!"

"There are other cousins, My Lord, but there is no doubt that Mr. Euan is the prior claimant."

Lord Alistair faced the fireplace and looked up at the painting above it of the Castle standing high above the sea, the heather-covered moors rising behind it.

As it was depicted with its turrets and towers, it was very impressive and exceedingly beautiful.

At the same time, he was well aware that he would feel dominated and threatened by his father's presence, and there would be also a sense of isolation, living in a world outside what to him was the real world and giving up everything which until now had made his life enjoyable.

Every instinct in his body told him he could not bear it, and yet his brain knew he had no alternative.

He could hardly survive with no money, living off his friends or asking his Harlow relatives to support him.

His mother's father was dead, and his uncle, now the Earl, had a large family of his own and had never been particularly interested in him.

What was more, he was far too proud with what Mr. Faulkner had called his "Scottish blood" to be a scrounger.

He turned from the window to face Mr. Faulkner.

"Very well," he said, "you win! How soon will we have to leave for Scotland?"

There was certainly not the triumph that Lord Alistair had expected to see in Mr. Faulkner's expression. In fact, the older man hesitated, and his eyes seemed apprehensive.

"What is it?" Lord Alistair enquired.

"It had been announced, My Lord," Mr. Faulkner replied, "that your brother the Marquis was to be married to Lady Moraig McNain!"

"Well?"

"His Grace has given his word that Lady Moraig should marry his eldest son to unite their Clans, which, as you are well aware, have been at loggerheads with each other for generations."

There was a silence that seemed to pulsate through the small Dining-Room before Lord Alistair said incredulously:

"Are you telling me that my father will expect me to honour this arrangement?"

"I was afraid this might upset you, My Lord," Mr. Faulkner replied. "But because His Grace considers it a question of honour, he will insist on it!"

Chapter Two

There was a long silence. Then, as if he thought the strain was unbearable, Mr. Faulkner said hastily:

"I hope, My Lord, you will now permit me to leave you, as I have several appointments to keep in London on behalf of His Grace."

Lord Alistair did not reply, and Mr. Faulkner went on:

"I have ascertained that there is a ship leaving Tilbury early tomorrow morning, which will carry us to Aberdeen, where His Grace's yacht will be waiting."

Still Lord Alistair was silent, and as if the expression on his face was intimidating, Mr. Faulkner bowed rather nervously and went from the room.

Only when he had gone did Lord Alistair realise that without being aware of it he had clenched his fists tightly in an effort at self-control.

Now he asked himself furiously, in a manner which seemed to burn through his whole body, how he could endure such a future.

It would be hard enough to accept the position as his father's eldest son and prospective Chieftain of the Clan, but to be married to some Scottish woman he had never seen was an humiliation that made him feel that any life, however impoverished, was preferable.

However, he was sure that Mr. Faulkner had not been

speaking lightly when he said that if he refused to return to Scotland, his father would disown him.

This would mean that all he would possess in the world would be the few hundred pounds a year that his mother had left him when she died.

While she had been living at home her father had not only provided for her but, as Lord Alistair knew, paid his School and University fees.

This had left the money which came from Scotland free for clothes, entertainments, and anything else he and his mother particularly fancied.

They had gone abroad together while he was still a boy, and when he was grown up he had visited many parts of Europe and enjoyed the experience.

To travel was expensive, and it was possible only because both his grandfathers had been so generous.

The idea of existing in the future without horses, without a comfortable flat like the one in which he now lived, and without the small appendages of wealth which became very precious when one lost them was unthinkable.

And yet, could any money compensate for living in the isolation of the Castle and being married to a woman who was doubtless gauche, plain, and badly educated?

When he thought of the intelligent men in politics and in the Social World whom he called his friends, and of the "Beauties" to whom he had made love, he felt himself shudder.

Then suddenly, almost as if a life-line were thrown to him, an idea came to his mind.

If he was married before he reached Scotland he could not be forced to become the husband of Lady Moraig, and there would be nothing his father could do about it.

It was not the answer to the whole problem, but at least it alleviated some part of the horror of what had been planned for him.

There was almost a smile on Lord Alistair's lips as he

realised that if he could persuade Olive to marry him, as he was quite certain she would be only too willing to do now that he was a Marquis, then he could pay back his father in his own coin by being able quite legitimately to defy his orders.

With a spring in his step he walked from the Dining-Room to his bedroom, where Champkins was waiting to help him into his coat.

It had only just arrived from Shultz, his tailor, and it fitted over his shoulders without a wrinkle.

It was in fact so smart that Champkins said with an undoubted note of admiration in his voice:

"This'll be one in the eye for Mr. Brummel, M'Lord, when he sees you!"

"I hope so, Champkins," Lord Alistair replied.

At the same time, he remembered how expensive the coat had been and that he owed Shultz quite a considerable amount of money.

Once again it was being hammered into his brain that as his father's heir he could meet all his bills without any difficulty.

But as a rebel and an outcast there would be every chance of his ending up in the Debtors' Prison.

"Are you going out, M'Lord?" Champkins enquired.

Lord Alistair nodded, and his valet handed him his high-crowned hat, a cane which had his crest on the gold knob, and his gloves.

He knew that in his tight-fitting champagne-coloured pantaloons, with his Hessians shining so brightly that they reflected like mirrors, and the points high above his chin, he looked exceedingly smart as he walked out of the flat and into Half-Moon Street.

Because he had given no orders the night before, his Phaeton, which had recently been delivered from the coach-builders, was not waiting for him.

Instead, Lord Alistair walked slowly towards Piccadilly, enjoying the sunshine because it was tempered with the dust of London, and enjoying the houses rising on each side of him because they were filled with people.

All too clearly he could see in his mind the long stretches of empty moors where only the grouse lived, and he could taste the salt on the sharp wind which would be blowing in from the sea.

As he strolled down Piccadilly, continually meeting acquaintances and being waved to by attractive women in their high-brimmed bonnets driving in open carriages, Lord Alistair was savouring everything he saw.

He felt a deep affection for the pavement under his feet, the trees in Green Park, and the roofs of Devonshire House silhouetted against the sky.

'This is my life. This is where things happen which affect the whole nation,' he thought. 'What shall I think about, talk about, and feel in the emptiness of the Highlands?'

Because it hurt him, he was determined that he would let nobody know yet of his changed circumstances.

Tomorrow he might be the Marquis of Kildonon, but today he was still Lord Alistair McDonon, the most admired, spoilt, pursued young man in the whole of the *Beau Monde*.

He guessed, although Mr. Faulkner had not said so, that one of the appointments his father's Comptroller would keep today would be in Fleet Street to have the news of his brothers' deaths reported in the London newspapers.

Tomorrow *The Times* and *The Morning Post* would undoubtedly headline such a tragedy, but today, Lord Alistair thought, there were still a few hours left in which he could be himself, and not his father's son, to be ordered about as if he were a raw recruit.

Thinking back into the past, he could hear his father's voice echoing through the corridors of the Castle and seeming to fill the big, high-ceilinged rooms.

When His Grace was in a rage it was as if the whole foundation of the Castle were shaken by a tempest, and as he grew older he watched his mother becoming more nervous, her face growing whiter, her eyes more apprehensive day by day.

She undoubtedly had a character and a strong personality of her own, but she was also extremely sensitive.

It had been impossible for her to go on living with a man who was obsessed with his own importance and behaved not only like a King but also like a tyrant.

When much later Lord Alistair was grown up, he realised how brave it had been of his mother to run away, afraid with a fear that was as violent as a dirk-thrust in her heart that she would be stopped and forcibly brought back.

But actually the Duke had been too proud to pursue her, and when he learnt that she had left secretly at dawn with her youngest son, Alistair, he had merely commanded everybody in the Castle never to speak of her and her name never passed his lips.

Only when he learnt that she had died did he assert his authority and insist that because she was the Duchess of Strathdonon, her body was to be brought back to lie with the bodies of previous Duchesses.

The Cemetery which was near to the Castle itself was surrounded by trees and a high wall to prevent the curious from peeping at their betters even though they were dead.

Lord Alistair had refused to meet the older members of the Clan who came to take the Duchess back to her last resting-place.

He had felt resentfully that it was just like his father to claim what he considered was his even after death.

He had therefore contented himself with mourning his mother publicly at a Service of Remembrance which took place in the Harlow family Church.

Now as he turned from Piccadilly into St. James's Street and saw the steps of White's Club just ahead, he knew that this was the place he would miss more than anything else when he was in the North.

The smartest and most exclusive Club in London, it was here that he could meet his friends at any time of the day or night.

At the moment it was filled with congenial souls who smiled at seeing him the moment he appeared.

Half-a-dozen voices called out a greeting as he entered the Coffee-Room, and he seated himself beside one of his closest friends, Lord Worcester, who asked:

"How are you feeling after last night, Alistair? I have a throat like a parrot's cage! It is the last time I shall ever take a drink in a brothel!"

"We were both fools," Lord Alistair agreed, "but the price we were charged for it should have ensured us a good wine."

"I suppose they thought that by that time we would not be very discriminating," Lord Worcester said. "What will you have now?"

A waiter took their orders, and Lord Alistair, sitting back in a comfortable leather armchair, felt as if he must etch the room and the faces of everybody in it firmly on his memory so that when he was in exile it would be a picture to remember.

He thought the same all through the excellent luncheon he and Lord Worcester ate together in the Dining-Room with its red walls, high windows, and gilt-framed paintings.

Then, earlier than Olive was expecting him, he allowed his friend who had an appointment with Harriet Wilson, the famous Courtesan, to drop him off in Park Street.

For the last two hours Lord Alistair had been restless in his anxiety to see Olive and make her agree to marry him at once.

He was quite sure that now that he had a coronet to offer, her love would outweigh every other obstacle and she would consent to come with him to Scotland.

Not perhaps tomorrow, that would be too much to ask, but within a few days.

He had to make her understand that it would be a mistake to antagonise his father more than he would be anyhow by the disruption of his plan.

"He can hardly blame me for already being married at my age," Lord Alistair argued to himself, "and it will be easy to make him believe that the marriage took place before the deaths of my brothers."

He knew he was asking a great deal of Olive.

Most important of all, because he was now in mourning, he would not be able to marry her as she would wish, in St. George's, Hanover Square, with the Prince of Wales present and a large Reception after the ceremony.

Although she was a widow and could not wear white, she would, Lord Alistair thought, in her inimitable way look breathtakingly beautiful.

The fact that she was marrying a future Duke would be accepted by everyone in the Social World as her right and no more than what was expected for her.

It would also be a satisfaction to know he had put Torchester's nose out of joint and also Harrowby's.

He would not only be married to the most beautiful woman he had ever seen, but one who undoubtedly, as she had declared over and over again, loved him with her whole heart.

It was not really surprising, Lord Alistair thought, when they were so well suited to each other, and the fire of their love-making was more intense and more passionate than that which he had known with any other woman.

However, it was not exactly the marriage he had envisaged, and he had an uncomfortable feeling at the back of his mind that he would never be completely confident that Olive would be permanently faithful to him.

Because many married women had been so willing for him to make love to them, Lord Alistair was very cynical about the chance of any woman, if she was beautiful enough, being faithful or loyal to one man for any length of time.

Somewhere, and it was connected with the empty shrine within his heart, there was the idea that he would wish his own wife not only to love him but to be shocked and affronted if any other man tried to touch her.

Then he twisted his lips as he told himself mockingly that it was asking too much.

Only if a woman was plain and boring, as he was sure Lady Moraig would be, was she likely to remain faithful to him alone until death divided them.

Deep in thought, he reached Olive's home without being aware of it, and raised his gloved hand to the shining knocker on the door.

It was opened immediately by a young footman wearing the somewhat flamboyant livery affected by the Beverley family.

Lord Alistair stepped inside before he asked the Butler, who knew him well, and who came hurrying over the marble floor:

"Is Her Ladyship at home, Bateson?"

"She's not back yet, M'Lord. But I understood Her Ladyship was expecting Your Lordship at four o'clock."

"I am early."

The Butler seemed to hesitate for a moment before he said:

"There's a young lady in the Drawing-Room also waiting to see Her Ladyship. She was not expected, so I don't suppose Her Ladyship will keep Your Lordship waiting for long."

"Then I will wait in the Card-Room."

"Yes, of course, M'Lord," the Butler replied, leading the way, "and I'll bring Your Lordship the newspapers."

"Thank you, Bateson."

Lord Alistair walked into an attractive Sitting-Room which rejoiced in the somewhat pretentious name of "Card-Room."

It adjoined the Drawing-Room, and when there were large parties there was room in it for four small baize tables or one large one for those who felt their evening was incomplete without a chance to gamble.

There were no tables now, and Lord Alistair settled himself in a comfortable armchair by the window, hoping that Olive would not be too long and resenting the fact that she had another appointment before he could talk to her about themselves.

Bateson brought him the newspapers, saying:

"I'll tell Her Ladyship you're here as soon as she arrives, M'Lord."

"Wait until her other visitor has left," Lord Alistair replied. "then make sure we are not interrupted. I have a matter of importance to discuss with Her Ladyship."

"Leave it to me, M'Lord."

The Butler went from the room, closing the door behind him.

Lord Alistair made no effort to pick up the newspapers. Instead, he stared ahead with unseeing eyes, wondering how Olive would react to what he had to impart to her.

He could not help feeling sure that she would be radiantly happy at the thought of being his wife, even if it entailed spending some months of the year in Scotland.

'She will sell this place,' Lord Alistair was thinking, 'and will open Kildonon House in Park Lane.'

It had always annoyed him that his father had closed the family Manor in London, which his grandfather had frequently used, and refused to allow either his wife or his sons to stay there.

Every time he passed it driving down Park Lane and saw its windows shuttered and the steps leading up to the door dirty and neglected, he felt irritated.

It was as if the dislike he had always felt for his father and his defiance of him were increased by this monument to his obstinacy and desire for isolation.

"He was born a century too late!" Lord Alistair had always said.

Twenty-five years after the Battle of Culloden, in 1746, the Chieftains had begun to neglect their Clans, and their sons had come South for their education and their amusement.

They had accepted the English as friends, enjoying the delights and entertainments of London as if they had never been defeated and humiliated.

The ancient authority of the Chiefs had been taken from them by the abolition of their heritable jurisdiction, which had given them the power of "pit and gallows" over their people.

The Clansmen had been stripped of the tangible manifestations of their pride, the carrying of arms was forbidden under the penalty of death, and the wearing of the tartan, the kilt, or plaid was an offence which involved transportation.

These cruel laws had later been rescinded, but Lord Alistair knew in his heart that they would never be forgotten.

He remembered reading recently that in Scotland, whenever there was news of a French victory, green firs were planted which symbolised freedom and liberty.

"Oh, God!" he said to himself with a sudden surge of irritation. "Have I got to listen to all that bitterness and fury against the English all over again?"

It had been an integral part of his childhood which he had learnt to forget, but now it seemed to surge up within him like a tidal wave, and he knew that if he was not careful he would be drowned in it.

He heard the sound of voices in the Hall and realised that Olive had returned.

Without thinking about it, he rose to his feet, then remembered with annoyance that she had another caller to see before she was free.

He heard her speaking to Bateson, then there was a click like that of a door opening, and he thought she had come to him first.

Then he realised that the door into the Hall was still shut, but the communicating door between the Drawing-Room and the Card-Room was ajar.

"You wanted to see me?"

It was Olive speaking.

"Y—yes . . . My Lady . . . I am desperately sorry to . . . bother you . . . but I have come to . . . you for help."

The voice that answered Lady Beverley was low and soft and, Lord Alistair thought, very frightened.

"For help?" The question was sharp. "Who are you?"

"My name is Arina Beverley."

There was a moment's pause while Lord Alistair was sure that Olive was looking surprised before she said:

"Do you mean to tell me that you are the daughter of Charles Beverley, my late husband's brother?"

"Y-yes . . . that is right."

"Then why have you come to see me?"

"Because I am desperate . . . absolutely desperate . . . My Lady. Although it may seem an . . . imposition, since we have never met before . . . I have nobody else to turn to . . . and I feel that because Papa was your brother-in-law . . . you would . . . understand."

"Understand what? I do not know what you are trying to say."

To Lord Alistair it seemed as if Arina Beverley drew in her breath.

"You are aware," she began after a little pause, "that my father . . . died two years ago."

"I believe my husband did mention it to me," Olive replied casually, "but as you know, because of your father's disgraceful behaviour in marrying your mother, the Beverley family cut him out of their lives."

"S-Sir Robert came to my . . . f-father's Funeral."

"Which I considered a very generous action on his part. Your father brought disgrace on the family name, and only a good Christian like my husband would have forgiven him after he was dead."

"At the same time," Arina said, "the . . . allowance Papa had always received first from his father . . . then from Sir Robert . . . ceased."

"Did you expect anything else?"

"It would have been . . . Christian to remember that the . . . living still need to be . . . cared for when the dead no longer . . . need help."

"That is not for you to say!" Olive retorted. "Tell me why you are here. I have no time to waste in arguments over your father's behaviour, considering that I never met him, and neither he nor your mother was of the slightest interest to me."

"Please . . . please . . . do not say that!" Arina begged. "I have . . . come to you for . . . help, because . . . my m-mother is . . . desperately ill. My father's death affected her very . . . deeply and now the Doctors say she must have an operation if she is to continue to . . . live."

"That is not my business!"

"My mother's name is Beverley . . . My Lady . . . as yours is . . . and all I am asking is that you will . . . lend me two hundred pounds, which will . . . pay for her to be operated on in a private Nursing-Home by a Specialist in the particular disease from which she . . . suffers."

There was silence, then Arina continued:

"I . . . I will pay it back . . . I swear I will pay it back however . . . long it may take me . . . but every day her operation is delayed . . . my mother grows worse!"

There were tears in the young girl's voice, but Olive's voice was sharp and hard as she replied:

"And how do you expect to repay this sum of two hundred pounds, except perhaps by walking the streets, although I doubt if even there you could raise such a large sum very quickly."

Arina gave a little cry of sheer horror.

"H-how can you . . . think of anything so w-wicked, so degrading?"

"Beggars cannot be choosers! Since that appears to be the only solution to your problem and you are not prepared to raise the money in such a way, I suggest you look elsewhere for help."

"Y-you . . . cannot mean . . . that!"

"I most certainly do mean it! You have no right to come here badgering me to provide money for a woman who should never have tempted my brother-in-law away from his family in the first place, and who is certainly no responsibility of mine."

"Please . . . Your Ladyship . . . please . . . try to understand . . . there is nobody else to whom I can turn for help and I . . . feel sure . . . that if Sir Robert were alive he would have . . . helped Mama."

Arina gave a little sob before she continued:

"When he spoke to me at the Funeral I knew . . . that despite the estrangement between the two brothers over the years . . . Sir Robert was still . . . fond of my f-father."

"If my late husband was a sentimental fool, I am not!" Olive snapped. "Now, as I have nothing further to say on the subject, I suggest you go back to your mother, and if she is ill get her into a Hospital."

"Even if there was a bed available in one of the free Hospitals," Arina replied in a strangled voice, "it would be . . . murder to send my mother into one . . . you have no idea of . . . the dirt . . . the disease which . . . flourishes in them . . . and the incompetence of the Doctors . . ."

"That is not my concern," Olive objected. "Leave now, and do not come back. If your mother dies, it is entirely her own fault, and she has nobody else to blame. I suspect actually she is receiving her just reward for the way she behaved in the past."

"How can you say anything so . . . cruel?" Arina cried. "My mother's only crime was that she loved . . . Papa as he loved her . . . and nothing else in the world . . . mattered to them."

"But now she is finding that money is a necessity!" Olive sneered. "Very well, I hope you find it, but it will not be from me!"

Lord Alistair heard Arina give an exclamation. Then he knew that she was crying.

Olive Beverley must have rung the bell, for he heard the door being opened and she said:

"Show this young woman out and see that she does not come back here again! I am going upstairs to change. Let me know when Lord Alistair arrives."

"But, M'Lady . . ."

As Bateson spoke there was a sudden thump, as if somebody had fallen down, and Lord Alistair heard him give an exclamation.

Without considering that he had been eavesdropping, Lord Alistair opened the communicating door into the Drawing-Room.

Olive had gone, but lying on the floor was a slight figure and Bateson was bending over it with an expression of concern on his face.

As Lord Alistair reached Arina's side, her eye-lids fluttered and she made what sounded like a murmur of apology.

"Brandy!" Lord Alistair said in commanding tones.

Bateson, as if suddenly realising that was the right solution, hurried through the open door into the Hall.

Lord Alistair went down on one knee and thought as he looked down at Arina Beverley that her appearance somehow matched her voice.

She had fair hair and was very slight, and as he saw the hollows in her cheeks and the pallor of her skin, he was sure that she was half-starved and had fainted not only from despair but from lack of food.

As her eyes widened and she stared up at him he saw that they were so large that they seemed to dominate her thin, pointed face.

They were not blue as might have been expected, but the pale green of a woodland stream, and her nose was very strange and, Lord Alistair thought, aristocratic.

Her lips were softly curved, but too thin, again from the first stages of starvation.

"I . . . I am . . . sorry!"

He could barely hear her voice, but somehow she managed to speak.

"It is all right," he said soothingly. "Lie still until the Butler brings you something to drink."

"I . . . I must . . . go."

"In a minute or two."

As he spoke, Bateson came hurrying back with a small glass of brandy on a silver salver.

Lord Alistair took it from him and, putting his arm round Arina, raised her a little from the floor, at the same time holding the glass to her lips.

She sipped, then shuddered as the fiery liquid coursed down her throat.

"No . . . more," she begged.

"Drink a little more," Lord Alistair said firmly.

As if she was too weak to argue, she obeyed him.

She shuddered again, but it was obvious that the darkness which had made her collapse had been swept away, and the colour came back into her cheeks.

"I am . . . sorry for being . . . so . . . foolish," she said in a frightened, hesitating little voice.

"I quite understand," Lord Alistair replied. "You have had a shock, and now I am going to send you back to your mother in a carriage."

"Oh . . . please . . . we cannot . . . afford it," Arina said quickly.

"You will not have to pay anything," he promised. "Let me help you up."

He knew that the brandy had already done its work, and he helped Arina to her feet, realising as he did so how light she was.

While she had seemed very small on the floor because she was so thin, when standing up she was in fact tall enough to be the perfect height for a young woman.

She was still a little unsteady and swayed as she stood, but Lord Alistair gave her his arm and she placed her hand in it.

With her other hand she pressed her plain bonnet firmly on her head and smoothed down her gown, made of a cheap cotton, which had become disarranged by her fall.

"A hackney-carriage!" Lord Alistair said to Bateson.

"Yes, of course, M'Lord."

He gave the order to one of the footmen, who hurried out through the front door into the street.

By the time Lord Alistair and Arina had walked very slowly to the top of the steps, a hackney-carriage had drawn up outside.

Only when they had reached the door of it did Arina take her arm from Lord Alistair's to say:

"Thank you . . . very much . . . you have been . . . very kind."

"I want you to give me your address," Lord Alistair said, "first so that I can tell the cabby where you live, and secondly because later in the day I will send you and your mother some food and wine."

"N-no . . . please . . . you must not . . . trouble yourself."

"It is something I want and intend to do!" Lord Alistair answered firmly. "All you need to tell me is your address."

"It is a lodging-house in Bloomsbury Square . . . it was the only place we could . . . afford . . . but we must leave it . . . tomorrow."

"And the number?"

"Number Twenty-seven . . . and thank you again for being so . . . kind to me."

Arina held out her hand as she spoke, and as it was ungloved, as he took it Lord Alistair felt her fingers were cold and trembled against his.

He gave the address and the fare to the cabman and the hackney-carriage drove off.

As he walked back up the steps he thought he would send Arina not only some food but also a little money, enough at any rate to make sure she would not starve for the next week.

Then he told himself ironically that if he had not decided to obey his father's command, it was something he could not have afforded to do.

He walked in through the front door and said to Bateson as he did so:

"Tell Her Ladyship I am here, and ask her to speak to me as quickly as possible."

"Very good, M'Lord."

Bateson started up the stairs and Lord Alistair walked into the Drawing-Room.

He saw the flowers and thought that what they had cost would have supplied Arina and her mother with quite a number of substantial meals.

Then he told himself that it was ridiculous for him to allow a strange young woman's problems to concern him at this moment when he was so deeply involved in his own.

The thing that really mattered was not whether two unknown women were starving because of some deplorable action in the past, but that Olive would be prepared to marry him by Special Licence.

He knew women well enough to realise that as regards getting married, nobody as distinguished as Olive would wish to be hurried over what to most women was the most important day in their lives.

But where he was concerned, marriage was not only imperative but must be immediate.

To wait longer would be to allow the Duke to suspect that he had married in defiance of his wishes, and that would certainly be the wrong way to start his new life as prospective Chieftain.

No, it was essential that his father should think he was already married when the summons to return to the North had reached him.

Mr. Faulkner was bound to be suspicious since he had not immediately protested that he was already married, but Lord Alistair knew that he had been very fond of his mother and of himself even as a boy, and so could be relied on, he hoped, not to betray him.

The whole plan was beginning to lay itself out in his mind so clearly that he might have been directing a movement of troops rather than of himself and of course Olive.

He had to wait for nearly a quarter-of-an-hour before she came into the Drawing-Room, looking exquisitely beautiful in a gown of glowing pink gauze so transparent that it revealed the exquisite curves of her figure.

It was the fashion among the Ladies of Fashion to dampen their muslins so that they clung closely to their figures, but Olive was skilful enough to choose materials that showed hers without such artificial aids.

As Bateson shut the door behind her, Olive stood for a moment as if to allow Lord Alistair to take in the picture she made.

Then she gave a little cry of delight and ran towards him with a grace worthy of any ballerina on the stage at Covent Garden.

"Alistair!" she exclaimed with delight. "It is so wonderful to see you!"

It flashed through Lord Alistair's mind that her voice when she was speaking to him was very different from the harsh tones in which she had addressed Arina.

Then her red lips were lifted to his, and the seductive expression in her half-closed eyes made it hard for him to think of anything but her loveliness.

"I have something to tell you," he said.

"And I have something to tell you."

"Mine is very important."

"What can be more important than that you are here and, for some reason I do not understand, have not yet kissed me?"

"I want to tell you something first."

"Then tell me, Alistair, and tell me quickly, as I want your kisses and a—great deal more."

The passion in her voice was unmistakable, and Lord Alistair thought it was exactly what he wanted to hear.

Slowly and in a way that was almost dramatic he said:

"My two elder brothers have been drowned, and I am therefore now the Marquis of Kildonon!"

For a moment it seemed that Olive thought she must have misunderstood him. Then as she stiffened, her eyes opening wider to stare at him, Lord Alistair said:

"It is true! And my father has sent for me to go North. So, my sweet, we have to be married immediately before we journey to Kildonon Castle and I present you to my father and the Clan."

He finished speaking, and still Olive seemed tongue-tied, until with a strange little cry that was hard to interpret she asked:

"Is this—true? Really—true?"

"I learnt of it myself only this morning, and it has been a great shock to me. But my first thought was that now we can be married, and I can offer you the strawberry-leaf coronet you have always craved."

To his surprise, Olive, instead of melting into his arms as he had expected, looked away from him before she said:

"I told Arthur Harrowby last night that I would give

him his answer this evening. That is why I told you to
come here now, so that I could inform you first that I
intend to—marry him."

"Now he will be disappointed," Lord Alistair said. "You
will marry me and we shall be together as we have always
wanted to be."

To his astonishment, Olive walked towards the table on
which was a huge bowl of Malmaison carnations.

She put out her hand to touch them, as if to feel they
gave her something. Then she said:

"It is too—late!"

"What do you mean—it is too late? If you have not
already accepted Harrowby, then all you have to do is tell
him that the answer to his question is 'no.' "

Olive did not answer, and Lord Alistair asked:

"Why are you not as pleased as I thought you would be?
You have told me often enough how much you love me."

"I do love you, Alistair, but marriage is one thing, love
is another."

"I do not understand," Lord Alistair said, and now his
eyes were hard.

"I am glad—very glad for your sake that you are now a
Marquis and one day will be a Duke," Olive said quickly,
still staring at the carnations. "But your Castle is in—
Scotland. It is a long—way away."

"There is also a house in London, which I have every
intention of reopening."

Olive did not speak, and now he put out his hands and,
grasping her shoulders, turned her round to face him.

"What are you thinking? What are you trying to tell
me?" he asked harshly. "Are you saying that after all your
protestations of love, you would rather marry Harrowby
than me?"

"You are hurting me!" Olive complained.

Lord Alistair gave her a little shake.

"Answer me!" he insisted. "I want to know the truth!"

"You are still—hurting me—and it is very cruel and—
unkind of you."

Lord Alistair suddenly took his hands away.

"So you have made up your mind," he said harshly. "You will marry Harrowby because he is so rich and because his house and Estates are in the South of England."

"Try to understand," Olive pleaded. "I love you, Alistair, of course I love you, but I should hate having to live in Scotland, where there is nobody to admire me, no Balls, no Opera—and besides, I have always disliked cold weather."

"And the love—the love you have professed so often—does not come into it?"

"I love you, I shall always love you," Olive insisted, "and there is no reason why our relationship should be any—different in the future from what it has been in the past. Arthur is a busy man, and I shall have a lot of time to—myself."

As she spoke Olive stepped towards Lord Alistair, and now her eyes had narrowed again, and as she spoke the last words her lips had an invitation on them.

Lord Alistair drew himself up, his eyes dark as agates.

"I congratulate you, Olive, for what in the past has been a very skilful and professional performance! It certainly convinced me of your sincerity."

His voice was like a whip-lash as he added:

"Let me also congratulate you on becoming the Marchioness of Harrowby, an hereditary Lady of the Bedchamber to the Queen, and undoubtedly a future leader of London Society! What is more, I am sure you will make a great number of credulous fools like myself very, very happy!"

As he finished speaking he took from the pocket of his waistcoat a key, which he threw down on the floor.

"The key into your garden," he added. "I am sure you will need it tonight, and do not forget to leave the window into this room ajar!"

As he finished speaking he turned on his heel. Then as he opened the door, Olive gave a little cry which seemed to be forced from her lips.

"Alistair!" she cried. "Alistair!"

Lord Alistair did not look around, but crossed the Hall, snatching up his hat from a chair.

As a footman opened the front door, he ran down the steps and was striding away down Park Street, saying as he did so, beneath his breath:

"Damn her! Damn her! Damn all women!"

Chapter Three

Lord Alistair walked briskly towards Half-Moon Street.

As he nearly reached it, still seething with anger, the sight of a shop which purveyed food made him remember his promise to Arina Beverley.

Because in some obscure way he felt that if he helped her he would be scoring off Olive, he went into Shepherd Market where there were a number of shops patronised by his Chef.

He stopped at a Butcher's shop which was known in that area for the excellence of its meat and ordered a number of different cuts of beef and mutton, besides a chicken.

When the man, knowing who he was, had taken his order respectfully, he asked:

"Anything else I can do for you, M'Lord?"

Lord Alistair hesitated.

It suddenly struck him that if he helped Arina even further, he would be showing up Olive for her meanness and the cruel manner in which she had refused to help a desperate girl who was actually her niece.

The Butcher was waiting, and after a moment Lord Alistair replied:

"Send them round to my flat immediately and put in

41

two pounds of butter and add some fruit and vegetables from the shop next door."

"It'll be a pleasure, M'Lord!"

Lord Alistair walked away, and for the first time since leaving Park Street he felt that the way Olive had behaved to her brother-in-law's child was not the manner in which he would want his wife to speak to anybody, let alone a relative.

Her behaviour had actually been a revelation, for he had never known her to be anything but charming, sweet, and to him passionately loving.

Now he thought that with her social mask off she appeared to be a very unpleasant character, and he blamed himself for not having realised it sooner.

He had in fact, because he was a Celt, always flattered himself that his instinct was infallible and it would be impossible for any man to cheat him or any woman to deceive him.

But he had been deceived by Olive, and he was aware that while she would not marry him, she still desired him as a lover and would make every effort if they met in the future to entice him back to her bed.

Now he understood why even in their wildest transports of desire, some critical faculty had prevented him from thinking that this was real love.

Olive was in reality greedy, avaricious, and ambitious to the point where she would marry the Devil himself if he could give her a coronet, wealth, and a position in Stylish Society.

As Lord Alistair walked up to his Sitting-Room on the First Floor, he saw that Champkins was packing his clothes into a large leather trunk.

Because he had given him no direct order, he asked:

"What are you doing? Who told you to pack for me?"

Champkins looked up from where he knelt beside the trunk.

"That Scottish gentleman returned after you'd left, M'Lord. He wanted to see you important-like and said he'd be back at six-thirty."

Lord Alistair's lips tightened but he did not speak, and Champkins went on:

"He tells me Your Lordship were leaving for Scotland tomorrow morning, an' it's going to take me all night to get all Your Lordship's clothes ready."

Lord Alistair bit back the words of fury that came to his lips.

It was bad enough that he had no alternative to obeying his father's orders, but that Faulkner should be so certain of his compliance made him more incensed than he was already.

Then he asked himself what was the point of kicking against the pricks.

He could stay in London and starve, or he could take his rightful place as the next owner of Kildonon Castle and the hundred thousand acres of Scottish land that went with it.

For the first time since he had heard of his brothers' deaths, Lord Alistair remembered the power his father had in the North, and that his mother had been right when she had said he behaved like a King.

He was indeed "Monarch of all he surveyed," and his people, despite the English laws, looked to him for justice. As far as they were concerned, he, as Chieftain, was the law.

"There are a great many things I shall want to alter," Lord Alistair told himself.

He knew that already in his mind he was accepting his new position, however much his heart rebelled against the penalties that went with it.

He stood in the Sitting-Room, thinking of how much he had enjoyed living here, how comfortable he had been, and how many delightful hours he had spent either with his men-friends or with some beautiful lady.

She would come to him after dark, heavily veiled, but daring enough to risk her reputation and her marriage because she loved him.

For Olive, what he now had to offer was not enough.

It was hard to believe it, and it was still harder to credit that after all her protestations of love, she preferred Harrowby.

"Damn her! I hope she rots in hell!" he exclaimed.

Then he felt it was even more infuriating that she should arouse such uncontrollable emotions in him.

There was a loud knock on the door, and as Champkins ran downstairs to answer it, Lord Alistair realised it was the hamper he had ordered for Arina.

As Champkins came back up the stairs, he met him, saying:

"All right, I know what it is. Go round to the Mews and tell Ben I want my Phaeton brought round immediately."

It was only ten minutes before the Phaeton was at the door.

This was another possession which was not yet paid for, and as he drove off with the hamper at his feet and Ben, his groom, sitting beside him, Lord Alistair thought that he would make sure his father paid for the privilege of having him back.

It would have been an enjoyment for him to drive his two superlative horses if he had not been thinking that he would have to decide whether he would have them sent to Scotland or whether he should sell them before he went.

Although, as he had told Olive, he planned to open Kildonon House in Park Lane, he was aware that he would have to have his father's approval to do so, and he had the uncomfortable feeling that the answer would be a categorical "No!"

"Curse it, I have to have some independence!" he muttered to himself.

He knew as he spoke that it was just bravado.

Once he was back at the Castle, everything would be as it had been in the past, a Kingdom ruled over tyrannically by a Monarch with one idea, and one idea only—his own importance and the greatness of Scotland.

Number 27 Bloomsbury Square was not difficult to find.

The house looked sleazy and greatly in need of paint, while the windows were dirty and so was the doorstep.

Because it looked so unsavoury, Lord Alistair for the

moment played with the idea of leaving the hamper for Arina and driving away.

Then he remembered that Olive had treated her as badly as she had treated him, and there was a cynical twist to his lips as he thought that he would let her know in a subtle way how generous he had been.

He knew he had only to tell a few of the gossips in White's that evening that he had learnt of the distressing state in which Olive's sister-in-law and niece were living for it to be a tit-bit which would fly on the air from lip to lip.

Everybody was aware that Sir Robert Beverley had left his wife a comfortable income for life, with doubtless a clause inserted that she lost it if she remarried.

This was so usual amongst the elderly husbands of pretty young wives that it had ceased to cause comment.

At the same time, Olive was at the moment, in the colloquial phrase, "well-heeled," and that she had refused to help her sister-in-law and her niece would certainly be ammunition for the women who were jealous of her and the men whose advances she had spurned.

There was a cruel twist to his lips and a hard expression in his eyes as Lord Alistair climbed down from the Phaeton.

Ben had already rung the bell and lifted down the hamper, and now he took his Master's place with the reins, preparing to walk the horses round and round the Square until they could start off again for home.

A slovenly maid, who looked as if she had been cleaning the soot from the chimney, came to the door.

"I wish to speak to Miss Arina Beverley," Lord Alistair said.

"You'll find 'er on th' third floor, Mister," the maid said, jerking a thumb up towards some narrow stairs that were badly in need of dusting.

"I suspect that is her bedroom," Lord Alistair said. "There must be somewhere else where I can talk to the young lady."

The maid looked at him in surprise. Then, obviously

impressed by his magnificent appearance, she said hesitatingly:

"There's th' mistress's Parlour, but 'er be oot at the moment."

"I feel sure she will not mind my using it," Lord Alistair said firmly. "Show me to it."

As if his air of authority left her defenceless and unable to withstand his command, the maid opened a door on the other side of the Hall.

Here there was a small, quite comfortably furnished Sitting-Room, over-cluttered with cheap paintings and the type of china sold by pedlars, but at least it was unoccupied.

"Fetch Miss Arina," Lord Alistair said as he walked in, "and take the hamper I have brought with me upstairs at the same time."

As he spoke he drew half-a-guinea from his waistcoat pocket and put it into the maid's hand.

She stared at it as if she thought she must be in a dream.

Then her face flushed with excitement.

"Yes, Mister, yes, Sir!" she said in a very different tone of voice. "Oi'll fetch th' young lady right away!"

She pulled the door to, and Lord Alistair heard her hurrying up the stairs with the heavy hamper as if she was afraid he might change his mind and demand his money back.

He was thinking that if he did not go to Scotland he would not be able to tip so generously on any future occasion.

Then his thoughts returned to Olive and the knowledge that what he was doing now would undoubtedly damage the picture she had created of her beauty, gaiety, and laughter, and of course her social superiority.

"The Marchioness of Harrowby!"

He spoke the words aloud and heard the sneer in his voice.

Then he told himself that he was wasting his time in letting his thoughts dwell on Olive, when he should be thinking of his own misery on being forced to marry a

Scotswoman from a Clan which he could remember as a boy had always been the enemy of the McDonons.

They had fought all through the centuries, warring against each other with raids in which they captured women and cattle.

He could therefore understand his father's desire to end the hatred and the malice that existed between his people. and the McNains.

"But not at my expense!" Lord Alistair exclaimed.

As he spoke, the door opened and Arina came in.

She had changed, he noticed, from the cotton gown she had been wearing when he had last seen her into one of white muslin which was limp from many washings.

The result was that it clung to her figure in a manner which Olive and other ladies of the Social World considered fashionable.

It was frayed in places, and, being experienced about women's clothes, Lord Alistair thought that when she had returned to her mother she must have changed out of her respectable gown to save it for better occasions.

She obviously had no idea that he himself would bring the food he had promised her.

She dropped him a small but graceful curtsey before she said:

"How can you be so . . . kind as to bring Mama and me that . . . huge hamper? I do not know . . . how to thank you."

"I always keep my promises," Lord Alistair replied. "I am glad it pleases you."

"P-pleases . . . me?" Arina repeated. "It is like a gift from . . . God . . . and I am sure it will make Mama feel . . . better."

"And you too," Lord Alistair said. "I realise you are very much in need of nourishment."

She smiled and he realised that when she did so her face was very lovely.

"I only took a quick look in the hamper before I came down to thank you," she said, "but already I am feeling very . . . greedy."

Looking at her, Lord Alistair thought that if she were not so thin that her cheek-bones stood out and her chin seemed far too sharp, she might be beautiful.

Then he corrected himself. She was beautiful now.

In fact, as he looked at her now more closely than when he had first seen her lying on the floor, he thought that her looks were quite unusual.

In some way he could not quite define, they were different from those of any other beautiful woman he had known. Yet she could, even in her cheap and frayed gown and with her hair unbound, take her place amongst them.

He had often thought to himself that the women he had known had formed a Picture-Gallery in his mind, which he could walk round, looking at their faces and knowing each particular point of beauty he had memorised about them.

One of his lady-loves had had eyes that always looked like pools of mystery, and it was sad to remember that beautiful though she was, he had found when he knew her well there was no mystery about her at all.

Another had lips that might have been chiselled by a Greek sculptor, and yet another had a nose that he was sure was more alluring than Cleopatra's!

One beautiful woman with whom he had been enamoured for a long time had red hair that echoed the flames she had ignited in him when he touched her.

But the beauty of Arina, he thought, would have been the beauty of somebody very young and Spring-like, if she had not been so thin and her skin pale and lustreless.

Her hair, while it was the colour of sunshine in the early morning, was limp because, like her body, it needed feeding.

Then he realised that because he was staring at her, Arina was looking at him apprehensively.

"Have I . . . said something . . . wrong?" she asked, faltering.

"No, of course not," he replied. "I was thinking about your difficulties and your plea for help from Lady Beverley, which I overheard because I was in the next room."

Arina flushed and looked away from him.

"It was . . . foolish of me to go to her . . . but I did not know . . . what else to do."

"I thought it was very wrong of her not to help you," Lord Alistair said in a sharp voice.

"I had hoped that she . . . would," Arina said simply, "but the . . . Beverley family never forgave Papa and Mama for . . . running away together."

"What did your father do that they considered so disgraceful?" Lord Alistair asked.

Then as an afterthought, before she could reply, he said:

"I suggest you sit down while we talk. After what you have been through, I am sure that you are tired."

"It is . . . kind of you to . . . think about me," Arina said, "but I am not so much tired as . . . anxious about Mama and what to do . . . about her."

As she spoke she sat down in one of the chairs by the hearth-rug, and Lord Alistair sat opposite.

"Tell me first about your father," he suggested.

Arina looked down at her clasped hands before she said:

"It happened a long time ago, but I suppose . . . nobody will ever . . . forgive him."

"What did he do?"

"He was engaged to be married to the daughter of the Duke of Cumbria."

Lord Alistair looked surprised.

He had known that the Beverleys were a respected family in the North, although he had rather suspected that Olive had exaggerated their importance, but he had not supposed that they moved in the same aristocratic circles as he did himself.

"I think," Arina was saying in her soft little voice, "that Lady Mary was more in love with Papa than he was with her, and he was rather pushed into the engagement by his parents and his brother, who were extremely impressed by the Duke."

Lord Alistair thought this explanation was very likely.

"Go on!" he prompted.

As if it encouraged her, she continued:

"Then, two weeks before the marriage was to take place, while the wedding-presents were pouring in, and it had been arranged for the Archbishop of York to marry them, Papa met my mother."

Lord Alistair felt that this was probably something that often happened, but few men would have had the courage to do anything about it.

"Mama said they fell . . . completely and . . . hopelessly in love," Arina went on, "and they both knew it would be impossible to go on living if they could not be together."

"So they ran away!"

"Yes . . . they ran away . . . and were married at Gretna Green, which is not very far from the Beverley Mansion in the North of Yorkshire."

"I can imagine how infuriated both the deserted bride and your father's family must have been."

"They were so angry that my grandfather never spoke to Papa again . . . and I have never seen my uncle until he . . . attended Papa's Funeral."

"I heard you say that to your aunt," Lord Alistair replied, "and also that your father received an allowance from his family."

"I have always . . . understood that it was his . . . mother who arranged that," Arina said, "and although it was very little to live on, we managed and were very . . . very happy . . . until Papa . . . d-died."

"Then the money stopped?"

"Yes."

"There was no reason given?"

"When I wrote to the Lawyers asking why it was . . . delayed, they replied that now that Papa was . . . dead, the Beverley family had no further obligation either to Mama or . . . to me."

Her voice seemed to die away on the words. Then she clasped her hands together as she said:

"We have sold . . . everything that was of any value and . . . if Mama is not operated on soon, the growth that is in her breast will . . . grow larger and she will . . . die! And although I have . . . prayed and prayed there . . . seems to be no way I can . . . raise the money now that Lady Beverley had refused to . . . help us."

The despair and terror in her voice seemed to vibrate through the small room, and after a perceptible pause, almost as if he debated the answer within himself, Lord Alistair said:

"I will give you the two hundred pounds!"

If he had fired a pistol at her, Arina could not have been more astonished.

For a moment she stared at him as if she thought she could not have heard him a-right. Then, without thinking, she said quickly:

"N-no . . . of course not . . . how could I ask you . . . a stranger, to give us . . . so much?"

"Shall I say that it is an act of Christian charity!" Lord Alistair replied, and he could not suppress the mocking note in his voice.

"But you must know . . . it will be a very . . . very long time before I would be . . . able to . . . pay you back. I shall have to find . . . some work that I can do . . . but it may not be . . . easy."

"I am prepared to wait."

"And you will really give it us . . . to save Mama's life? How can I thank you? How can I . . . tell you how wonderful it is for you to . . . answer my prayers?"

Her voice was very moving, and now there were tears in her green eyes, which made them look so beautiful that Lord Alistair found himself staring at her in astonishment.

Then as he did so, an idea came to him that was astounding and at the same time so outrageous that for a moment he found it difficult to grasp.

Yet, when he did so, it seemed as if he too had received the answer to a prayer.

He bent forward in his chair.

"Listen," he said, "I have an idea. If you need my help, I, as it happens, need yours."

"I will certainly help you . . . if I can do so. You know I

would do . . . anything after you have been so kind . . . so incredibly . . . kind."

"Very well," he said, "but just answer a question. If your mother goes into a Nursing-Home, where will you go?"

"I thought that if the Doctor would take her, as he said he would, I would try to find a cheap room somewhere nearby so that I could be beside her."

Arina paused, then continued:

"But he said that if I could find a little more . . . money, he could give me a room in the Nursing-Home. Although I have not yet suggested it, I thought I might be able to . . . help there in some way . . . perhaps by doing . . . house-work . . . so that I need not be so . . . greatly in his debt."

Lord Alistair had listened attentively, and now he said:

"I have a better suggestion and one which I want you to consider very carefully."

"What . . . is it?"

"I have a part for you to play, almost as if you were on a stage, although you will not be acting in a Theatre."

Arina looked puzzled but she did not speak, and he went on:

"I suggest you leave your mother in the Doctor's hands, and perhaps that would save her from worrying about you while she is ill."

"What do you . . . want me to . . . do?"

"I want you to come with me to Scotland," Lord Alistair replied, "on a visit which will take some little time, but if you will act the part that I require of you, I will pay for your mother's operation."

Arina made a little sound of happiness but did not interrupt, and he went on:

"There will also be enough to ensure that after it is over, she can convalesce in comfortable circumstances, and when you return to her you will both be able to afford to be properly nourished."

"It sounds . . . too wonderful!" Arina whispered. "But suppose I cannot do what you . . . want?"

"It will not be easy," Lord Alistair answered, "but I feel somehow you will be successful in convincing the people you will meet that you are the person you are pretending to be."

Arina looked puzzled before she asked:

"I have to . . . pretend to be . . . somebody else?"

"You will act the part of my wife!"

Lord Alistair spoke the words slowly and distinctly. He saw Arina stiffen and again stare at him as if she could not believe what she had heard.

"Y-your . . . wife?"

Her voice trembled on the words.

"Just as you are in a difficult position, so am I," Lord Alistair said. "What is not yet publicly known is that my elder brothers are dead. I am therefore now the Marquis of Kildonon!"

He paused expecting her to look impressed, but her expression was one of sheer astonishment as he continued:

"My father, the Duke of Strathdonon, has ordered me back to Scotland, and once there he intends me to take up the responsibility that my eldest brother had assumed before he died, and marry the daughter of the neighboring Chieftain, with whom we have always been at war. You may not understand it, but the word of any Chieftain in Scotland is equivalent to a vow made in Church."

"I do . . . understand . . . that," Arina answered.

"You will therefore realise that I would find it almost impossible to refuse to marry this woman whom I have never seen. So, the best way of avoiding a travesty of a marriage would be for me to arrive in Scotland with a wife."

"Yes . . . I can see that is your . . . only way . . . out."

Lord Alistair was aware that Arina was quicker-witted than he had expected, and he said:

"I am supposed to leave tomorrow morning, and once I have reached my father's Castle there will be no escape."

"I . . . I could not go tomorrow morning!"

"No, I quite understand that."

"Besides," Arina went on before he could say any more,

"I am not sure I am the . . . right person to do . . . this for you . . . I might . . . fail you . . . and . . . I would not look right."

Lord Alistair smiled.

"Like all women, you are thinking about your clothes," he said. "But I promise you that you will be dressed as would be expected of my wife."

"B-but . . . I could not . . . pay for it."

"I will do that, and if you have any scruples about accepting clothes from me, may I explain that every Theatrical Producer expects to dress his Leading Lady."

He spoke almost jokingly, but Arina did not smile.

"I want to . . . help you," she said, "but I am sure this is not . . . right from your point of view."

"Anything that will save me from having to marry a Scottish woman whom I have never seen will be right for me," Lord Alistair said firmly.

"A-and what . . . happens later?" Arina asked. "I shall have to . . . go back to Mama?"

This again, Lord Alistair thought, was a sensible question.

"We will have to work that out very carefully," he said, "and I was thinking that perhaps when the danger of my having to marry in Scotland was over, you might disappear."

"Yes . . . of course," Arina agreed. "Nobody would be . . . interested in what . . . happened to me anyway."

"You will come South to see your mother," Lord Alistair said slowly, as if he was planning it out for himself. "You will be ill and send for me. After I have joined you in the South, I can inform my father or anybody else who is interested that you have died."

"And they will . . . believe . . . you?"

"We shall have to make sure they do," Lord Alistair said firmly.

There was silence. Then he said:

"If you agree to do this for me, I will give you not the two hundred pounds for which you have asked, but five hundred. This will be deposited in the Bank for your mother to draw on, and after our arrangement has come to an end I will see that you are paid monthly a sufficient amount of money to keep you in more or less the same circumstances as you enjoyed in your father's lifetime."

He was quite certain from what Arina had said that this would not be a great drain on his resources, and it should be easy for him as the Marquis of Kildonon to appropriate such funds from the large allowance he was quite certain his father would allow his heir.

Although he had no idea of the exact extent of his father's fortune, he had always assumed that he was a very wealthy man and that when many Scottish Chieftains had become impoverished after the ruthless repression of the rising of the Young Pretender, the Duke's income came from various other sources that were not affected by the poverty in Scotland.

"You and your mother will be looked after until such time as you are able to marry a rich man," he finished.

"I think that is most unlikely," Arina replied, "since we have always lived very quietly, and our friends, although they are loyal and kind, have mostly been as poor as we were ourselves."

She paused. Then a smile seemed to illuminate her face as she said:

"But we were happy . . . and that was all that . . . mattered."

"Of course," Lord Alistair agreed. "But now, Arina, we must return to making plans and do so very quickly. How soon can your mother go into the Nursing-Home?"

"At once . . . if we have . . . the money. That was why I went to see Lady Beverley . . . because every day that Mama is not operated on, the . . . tumour will grow . . . bigger and get . . . worse."

She spoke very quietly, but Lord Alistair heard the terror in her voice.

"Then I suggest you take your mother to the Nursing-Home first thing in the morning," he said, "but do not tell her what you are about to do, as it would worry her. Just say that Lady Beverley has not only lent you the money for the operation but has most kindly arranged for you to stay with friends who live outside of London."

"I am sure Mama will . . . believe that," Arina said, "because she is so weak and ill at the moment that she does not think . . . very clearly."

"Then that makes it all the easier," Lord Alistair agreed. "I suggest that once your mother is in the Nursing-Home, you come back here, where I will collect you and we will buy your 'trousseau' for your journey to Scotland."

Arina did not reply and her eyes dropped before his, and he knew she was embarrassed at the idea of his buying her clothes.

It seemed a little thing when he was also paying for her mother's operation, but it made him understand as no words could have done that she had been properly brought up.

She was not only a Lady by birth but was educated in the conventional manner, which was something he would want in the woman who was pretending to be his wife.

There was a silence before he said:

"I must warn you that we have to guard against something which actually I have only at this moment remembered."

"What is that?"

"In Scotland there is a law known as a 'Marriage by Declaration Before Witnesses.' It means if two people assert, in the presence of others, that they are married, then they are in fact legally joined to each other."

Arina started before she said:

"Then what can we do if you present . . . me as your . . . wife and I agree? It might be very . . . difficult for you in the . . . future."

"It will be difficult only if you do not abide by our arrangement," Lord Alistair replied. "That is why I think we should draw up an agreement, which we will both sign, saying that you are acting a part under my instructions and that neither of us will claim later, whatever the circumstances in which we find ourselves, that we have become legally man and wife."

"It sounds, My Lord, as if you suspect that . . . I might not . . . abide by our arrangement," Arina said.

Once again he thought how quick-witted she was in understanding that he was safe-guarding himself against any demands she might make of him in the future.

"I was not thinking of your attitude over this," he said untruthfully, "or my own, but that somebody might want to make trouble once you have left me."

He saw the expression of relief on her face and thought she was very sensitive and he would have to treat her carefully.

Now she said a little hesitatingly:

"I would be very . . . pleased to sign such an agreement as you call it . . . and to assure you . . . My Lord . . . that never in any circumstances . . . would I be so ungrateful as to do . . . anything you did not wish."

"Thank you," Lord Alistair said. "I will bring it back with me tomorrow and make quite certain it is legally phrased."

He rose to his feet as he spoke and Arina rose too.

Then, as if she was suddenly aware of what she had committed herself to, she said:

"You are quite . . . quite certain I can do this for you? You do understand that I know nothing of the . . . Social World in which you live. I shall . . . make mistakes . . . and perhaps you will be . . . ashamed of me."

"I will see to it that you do not," Lord Alistair assured her, "and if you are grateful to me, I am very grateful to you, Arina. You must know how degrading and humiliating it would be for me to be married in such circumstances."

"Yes . . . of course . . . and I feel Papa would have understood that you would do anything to . . . escape."

"As he escaped," Lord Alistair said with a smile, "and I think it was very brave of him."

"You really. . .think that? You are not . . . appalled and horrified as his family were?"

"No, of course not! I think he did everything possible and it is disgraceful that he should have suffered for so many years for what most people would consider a very romantic and honourable action."

Arina's eyes seemed to hold the light of a thousand candles in them.

"H-how can you be so . . . understanding and . . . so kind?" she asked. "I only wish Papa could hear you say that . . . and when Mama is . . . b-better . . . I will tell her."

"Yes, you must do that," Lord Alistair agreed, "but not at the moment. It would be a mistake for her even to hear my name in case she . . . talks about us."

"She would not do that if I asked her not to," Arina answered, "but because she is ill, it would be best not to worry her."

She looked away in an embarrassed manner as she added:

"I think . . . Mama would . . . disapprove of what I am doing, but as you know . . . there is no other way I can help her . . . and I was desperate until . . . you came."

"You have not told your mother that Lady Beverley refused your request for help?"

"Actually I have not told Mama even that I went to see her. I thought if she said 'yes,' it would be a wonderful surprise, but that if she refused it would be depressing."

"That was sensible of you," Lord Alistair approved, "and it makes it easier for us to do what we have to do."

He smiled at Arina in a way that many women had found irresistible as he said:

"Now go upstairs, give your mother something to eat, and eat sensibly yourself. I have just realised that I forgot the wine I promised you, but perhaps it would be a mistake at the moment, and I will make up for it on our voyage to Scotland."

"Thank you," Arina said, "but we have everything we want, and I hope I can persuade Mama to eat. I know it will give her the strength to go into the Nursing-Home tomorrow."

Lord Alistair drew two notes of fifty pounds each from his pocket and put them down on a table which was laden with potted plants.

"Give this to the Surgeon," he said, "which is half of his fee. The rest I will let you have tomorrow."

He added a number of gold sovereigns, saying as he did so:

"Take your mother to the Nursing-Home in a comfortable carriage and tell it to wait so that it can bring you back here. I will call for you at about noon and pay what you owe the Landlady."

Tears fell from Arina's eyes as she looked at the money. Then she said in a broken little voice:

"I . . . I cannot . . . believe that this is . . . really happening . . . and I am not . . . dreaming."

"I promise you it will not vanish like fairy-gold," Lord Alistair said. "Now do exactly as I say, Arina, and after I have collected you tomorrow, you can leave everything in my hands until you return South to find your mother recovered from her operation, and you can be together with no more desperate problems."

He put his hand on her shoulder.

"Your prayers are answered for the moment," he said, "but you still have to keep on praying."

"I will . . . pray . . . and thank God for . . . you," she said in a strangled voice.

He smiled at her and went from the Sitting-Room, shutting the door to give her time to collect herself and the money from the table before she went upstairs.

Outside, his Phaeton had just completed its fifth turn round the Square.

He climbed into it and took the reins from his groom.

Then as he whipped up the horses and started to drive swiftly back towards Mayfair, he was thinking once again how he could hurt Olive.

He rehearsed the exact words he would utter later in the Club, which would be repeated and repeated as if by a swarm of bees carrying poisonous pollen to every chattering tongue in the *Beau Monde*.

Chapter Four

Mr. Faulkner had been waiting only twenty minutes when Lord Alistair returned to his flat.

During the last part of his drive he had stopped concentrating on Olive to think of what he should say to his father's Comptroller.

There was a grim expression on his face as he walked up the stairs and into the Sitting-Room. Mr. Faulkner, who had been reading a newspaper, hastily put it down and rose to his feet.

"Good-evening, My Lord."

Lord Alistair walked to his desk and placed on it some letters which he had picked up in the Hall as he entered the building. Then he said in a somewhat aggressive tone:

"I understand that you have told my valet that I shall be leaving with you for Scotland tomorrow morning."

"I am sorry if it was information Your Lordship did not wish me to divulge," Mr. Faulkner replied slowly, "but I understood when I left you this morning that you had agreed to come back to Scotland, which meant we should leave as soon as it is possible."

"I agree with you," Lord Alistair replied, "but actually it is impossible for me to leave tomorrow, and I cannot believe that a delay of twenty-four hours will be of world-shattering importance."

He spoke mockingly and thought Mr. Faulkner looked surprised.

"Sit down, Faulkner," he went on. "I have something to tell you."

Mr. Faulkner did as he was told, and now there was an expression of apprehension in his eyes.

It suddenly struck Lord Alistair that it was strange, considering his father's bullying ways, that Faulkner, who was a very intelligent and well-educated man, should be so devoted to him.

It was something he had never considered before, and because he found it rather touching that after all these years Mr. Faulkner should be so concerned with the McDonon family, his voice softened and he imparted his news in a rather different manner from what he had intended.

"I am afraid," he said, "that what I have to tell you, Faulkner, will come as somewhat of a shock, and it is obviously something which has never crossed your mind, but I am in fact a married man!"

Mr. Faulkner stared and exclaimed:

"Married, My Lord? Your father has no idea of it!"

"Why should he have?" Lord Alistair enquired. "He has not concerned himself with me since I was twelve."

"His Grace, your father, has not only been interested in your well-being but has received reports about you regularly."

Lord Alistair stared at him.

"Are you telling me," he said after a moment, "that my father has spied on me?"

Mr. Faulkner looked a little uncomfortable.

"That is a harsh word, My Lord, for what I prefer to think of as a paternal interest on the part of His Grace in his youngest son."

"I can hardly believe it!" Lord Alistair ejaculated, then he laughed. "It is the old story, is it not, Faulkner? The big spider never lets the little spiders go. While I believed I had completely cut myself off from my father, the Clan, and the problems of Scotland, he still has woven his web round me and there is no escape."

He thought that was so true that it was surprising he had not thought of it before.

Of course, the very fact that the Duke had continued to give him an allowance after his mother's death might have alerted him to the idea that his father thought one day he might return to the fold, either willingly or because, as it had turned out, he was obliged to do so.

His thoughts were interrupted by Mr. Faulkner with the question:

"Did Your Lordship really say you are married?"

"Yes, Faulkner, that is what I told you! But the reason my father's spies have not ferreted it out is that it was a secret marriage. Even my valet, who is now packing, on your instructions, has no idea that I have a wife."

"But you will bring her to Scotland with you, My Lord?"

"Naturally! And you now understand why it will be impossible for me to marry Lady Moraig McNain."

For several seconds Mr. Faulkner did not speak, and Lord Alistair said with some satisfaction:

"It will doubtless upset my father's plans for me, but of course there is nothing I can do about it unless I commit bigamy."

He spoke jokingly, but Mr. Faulkner did not smile.

"I will not pretend to you, My Lord, that it is not a shock," he said after a perceptible pause. "But of course the Marchioness of Kildonon will be welcome as your wife and I hope she will acclimatise herself to Scotland and the Castle."

"That remains to be seen," Lord Alistair answered loftily. "But you can understand that because my wife, like my valet, has to pack, it will be impossible for us to leave until the day after tomorrow."

He saw by the expression on Mr. Faulkner's face that he was glad it was to be no later. Then he asked, in a tone of voice which was undoubtedly apprehensive:

"Would it be impertinent to ask Your Lordship why your marriage has had to be a secret?"

Lord Alistair's eyes twinkled.

He knew his father's Comptroller was thinking that perhaps he had married an actress or a woman who was not acceptable to the Social World and was already wondering what the Duke would do about it.

However, Lord Alistair had expected such a question and had already thought of an answer, remembering when he was at Oxford one of his friends saying:

"If you are going to tell a lie, it should always be as near to the truth as possible so that it sounds credible."

It was a piece of advice that Lord Alistair had followed, and he said now:

"My wife is in deep mourning for her father. As she comes from a distinguished and well-known family in Yorkshire, it would be, as you can imagine, almost an insult to the dead that she should marry before the year of mourning is over."

He thought Mr. Faulkner drew a breath of relief before he said:

"Of course I understand, My Lord. That means there should be no publicity about your marriage until some months after you have reached Scotland."

"That was what I thought myself," Lord Alistair replied, "which reminds me—I imagine, while you have been in London, you have notified the newspapers of the deaths of my brothers."

"Yes, My Lord! It will be in *The London Gazette, The Times*, and *The Morning Post* tomorrow morning."

"Then, under the circumstances, the sooner we leave for Scotland the better," Lord Alistair said. "I can assure you that my wife is considering my interests as well as her own in promising she will be ready to sail with such inconvenient haste."

"I am very grateful, My Lord. I shall greatly look forward to meeting Her Ladyship."

As Lord Alistair rose to his feet, Mr. Faulkner said:

"I will go at once to cancel our passages for tomorrow and transfer them to another ship, which I happen to know will be leaving on the tide on Thursday about noon. Will Your Lordship require one or two cabins?"

"Two!" Lord Alistair said quickly. "If the sea is rough, which it invariably is, one has no need of spectators."

Mr. Faulkner hesitated.

"If Her Ladyship is a bad sailor, perhaps Your Lordship would prefer to travel by road. It will of course take a great deal longer, but I have always believed that women are more prone to seasickness than men."

"It is something I have never considered," Lord Alistair replied. "But as the long drive would be tiring and unbearably boring, I am sure my wife would prefer to brave the waves rather than bad roads, broken-down horses at the Posting-Inns, and inevitably the final menace of a Scottish mist."

Mr. Faulkner permitted himself to give a short, dry laugh.

"Your Lordship's eloquence confirms my opinion that the shorter the journey between London and Kildonon Castle, the better for us all."

"Very well, Faulkner, see to it!"

Lord Alistair escorted the elderly man to the door and only when he had left did he remember that he had not offered him a drink.

"I have too much to do!" he excused himself, and went to his desk.

It took him some time to write out first a draft and then the final document that he intended Arina to sign the following morning.

She did not seem the type of woman who would resort to blackmail, but one never knew, and after he had been so disillusioned by Olive he was not prepared to take any chances.

Even to think of how mistaken he had been about Olive's feelings for him brought the frown back between his eyes and set his lips in a tight line.

He was hating her because it was the first time a woman had not been prepared to give him everything he asked of her.

He was sure that the many protestations of love he had received in the past had been sincere, and there were at least half-a-dozen women he could name who, had they been in Olive's shoes, would have been only too eager for him to put a ring on their finger.

He told himself that his feelings were more those of hurt pride than of a broken heart. But that did not make him feel any kinder towards Olive, and when, nearly two hours later and gorgeously arrayed in his evening-clothes, he drove in a hackney-carriage to White's, he was once again plotting how he could hurt her most.

He walked into the Club and immediately met three of his closest friends.

"We wondered if you would be with us tonight, Alistair," one of them remarked. "Come and have a drink. James says he has an almost certain winner for Ascot next week. He will want to tell you about it."

"It is something I am very eager to hear," Lord Alistair replied.

They walked to the bar, but before they reached it they found a number of other cronies drinking champagne and were invited to join them.

They had only just sat down when Lord Alistair, who was facing the door, saw someone come into the room and felt himself stiffen.

It was the Marquis of Harrowby, and he thought he was the last person he wished to meet at this particular moment.

Lord Worcester also saw him and remarked:

"There's Harrowby! Shall I ask him to join us?"

Before Lord Alistair could reply, the Marquis saw Lord Worcester and walked towards him. When he reached the circle of friends, he said:

"Nothing could be better than that you should all be here. You can help me celebrate."

"Help you celebrate what?" Lord Worcester enquired.

"My engagement!" the Marquis replied quietly. "Lady Beverley has accepted me."

There was a moment of silence, which was one of surprise, then a cheer went up. Congratulations were on every man's lips as they lifted their glasses to toast both the Marquis and Olive.

It struck Lord Alistair that this was the one love-affair in which he had been so discreet, at Olive's special request, that it had never crossed any of his friends' minds that he might be upset by the news.

He thought, as he too raised his glass and drank the expected toast, that he had acted his part very skillfully, as he hoped Arina would act hers.

Nevertheless, in all the turmoil and excitement which followed Harrowby's announcement, there was no chance for him to speak in any derogatory way of Olive, and if he had done so it would not have been well received.

'It will keep,' he thought to himself.

He decided too that after all it would be a great mistake for any of his friends to know of Arina's existence.

Only after they had all dined together and the Marquis, having had a great deal to drink, had been pompous and far too long-winded in his conversation, did Lord Alistair think as he drove home that Olive would, in her marriage itself, receive quite sufficient punishment for her behaviour.

Firstly, she would undoubtedly be bored, for the Marquis was a very boring man.

Secondly, Lord Alistair thought, unless he was a very bad judge of character, even her beauty could not arouse the fire and passion which he had found irresistible and which to Olive herself was the very breath of life.

'She will be bored, bored, bored!' he thought with satisfaction, and was quite certain that sooner or later she would use every art and wile in her repertoire to entice him back to her.

"Shall I see you tomorrow?" Lord Worcester asked when Lord Alistair said good-night.

He had already received invitations to visit a Dance-Hall, a House of Pleasure, and to take a pretty ballerina from Covent Garden out to supper.

"I shall be busy tomorrow," he answered. "And you will not see me for some months."

"Some months!" Lord Worcester exclaimed. "Why not?"

"I have to go to Scotland," Lord Alistair replied casual-ly. "You will know the reason when you read your newspapers tomorrow morning."

"What has happened?" Lord Worcester questioned. "Tell me about it!"

"You will learn soon enough."

"I cannot understand why you are being so mysterious!"

"It will give you something to think about!"

Refusing to say any more, Lord Alistair hurried down the steps and into the carriage which one of the porters from the Club procured for him.

As he rode back to his lodgings, he was thinking of how much there was to do before he could leave for a new life, which he was quite convinced would be one of utter misery.

"Dammit," he said aloud. "Why could I not have gone on as before? I was happy, while now I have to face my father, the boredom of Scotland, and a pretence marriage."

The idea came to him that the latter, strange as it might be, might in fact be a saving grace. At least it would give him something to think about.

It would be amusing to pull the wool over his father's eyes and to circumvent his plans of marrying him to a McNain. He would have to keep very alert to see that neither he nor Arina was caught out.

The whole idea made him think of the pranks he had played as a School-boy and the mischief he and his friends had got up to at Oxford, when they had been pursued by the Proctors and severely reprimanded by their Tutors.

Once again he was up to mischief, although it was certainly more serious than anything in which he had been involved in the past.

There was a faint smile on Lord Alistair's lips as he entered his lodgings. He went up the stairs, thinking that he was earlier than usual and Champkins would be sur-prised to see him.

However, as he reached the top step, his valet came out of his bedroom to meet him, saying in a low voice:

"There's a lady to see you, M'Lord. She's waiting in the Sitting-Room."

"A lady!" Lord Alistair exclaimed.

It flashed through his mind that it must be Arina and she had come to tell him she had changed her mind. Or perhaps her mother was already dead and there was no reason now for her to need the money so desperately.

Then, as the questions in his mind kept him silent, Champkins added:

"This lady's not been here before, M'Lord. She's heavily veiled. She came in a carriage with two horses and smells of French perfume."

There was no doubt that Champkins was impressed by the visitor and it was quite obviously not Arina.

Lord Alistair did not reply.

He merely slipped his satin-lined cape from his shoulders, handing it with his tall-hat to his valet before he walked to the Sitting-Room and opened the door.

Although it was only dimly lit by a few candles, there was no need for more than one glance at the woman who rose from the sofa as he entered.

For a moment Lord Alistair could hardly believe his eyes. Then as he shut the door behind him he exclaimed:

"Olive! What the devil are you doing here?"

She came towards him. Her evening-gown was cut with such a low décolletage and was so transparent that she might as well have been naked.

"How could you leave me so cruelly?" she asked.

She walked forward until she was standing close against him, but Lord Alistair did not put out his arms.

"I have just left your future husband at the Club," he said coldly. "I congratulated him warmly on his engagement, and I am quite convinced, Olive, that you have chosen a man to whom you are very well suited."

The way he spoke was insulting, but Olive only gave a little laugh.

"Darling, you are jealous," she said. "And I adore you for it! Oh, Alistair, my sweet, how do you think I could lose you?"

For a moment Lord Alistair thought she had changed her mind and intended to say that she would marry him after all. But as she lifted up her arms and he saw the passion in her eyes and the invitation on her lips, he understood.

"No!" he said sharply, moving away from her.

He walked to his desk and as he did so he wondered if perhaps he had left there the contract he had drawn up earlier in the evening between himself and Arina. Olive would have had no compunction about reading it.

To his relief, he remembered that it was something he had not wished Champkins to see and had therefore locked it in a drawer, and the key was at this moment in his pocket.

He stood looking down at the blotter. Then Olive was beside him, slipping her hand into his.

"Try to understand, darling," she begged. "Marriage is one thing—love is another. That is what all men believe, so why should a woman be different?"

She waited for him to reply and as he did not do so she went on:

"I love you as I have never loved anyone before. My lips yearn for you and my body burns for you. What does it matter what my name is?"

"It matters that you will not do what I have asked you to do," Lord Alistair replied sharply.

Even as he spoke it flashed through his mind that after all she was right. What did it matter to him whether she was married to him or not? What she was offering was something it was unlikely he would ever receive from his wife.

Quite suddenly his attitude to her changed, and he was intelligent enough to realise that he had been right in thinking he was angry with her because she had damaged his pride, but not his heart.

He turned now and there was a smile on his lips and the frown had gone from between his eyes.

"What do you think the noble Marquis would say if he knew where you were at this moment?" he enquired.

"It is something he will never know," Olive replied, "either tonight or in the future."

Now, as if she sensed his change of mood, she moved a little closer and put her arms round his neck.

"Why think about tomorrow or the day after, or the day after that?" she asked. "I am here tonight. No-one will disturb us, and I want you, Alistair. I want you as I have never wanted a man before."

The passion in her words seemed to throb on the very air, and slowly, as if he mocked at himself for giving in to her, Lord Alistair put his arms round her.

Then, as he bent his head and his lips found hers, he kissed her roughly, almost brutally, as if he punished her for the anger she had made him feel.

As she clung to him closer and closer, he felt the fire that she had invoked in him so often before rising to burn through his body, sweeping away everything but his fiery desire for the softness of her, while the exotic fragrance of her perfume seemed to beguile his senses and he could no longer think.

"I want you! I love you! Oh, Alistair, I love you!"

Even while some cynical part of his mind that seemed very far away told him she was lying, automatically he picked her up in his arms and carried her across the room to the sofa.

*   *   *

Lord Alistair, driving his Phaeton, reached 27 Bloomsbury Square at exactly noon the following morning.

He was aware when he left his flat that the pile of luggage in the Hall had grown since he had last seen it, and now there were no fewer than six large leather trunks and the same number of small ones, making a mountain of baggage, which he felt would surprise Mr. Faulkner if no-one else.

He was about to tell Champkins that he had no need of so much when he remembered that he was moving his residence from London to Scotland and it would certainly be some time before he could return to patronise the tailors, who were acknowledged to be better at their trade than any others in the world.

What was more, although he had not told Champkins that they would not be returning to this particular flat, he had the idea that the valet was already aware of it.

Champkins had been with him ever since he had left Oxford, and although at times he had behaved rather like a protective Nanny, he was always loyal and trustworthy.

For the first time Lord Alistair wondered if Champkins would be able to tolerate Scotland any more than he would be able to himself.

He decided that when he returned he would tell Champkins that now he had packed all his clothes, he must arrange to put everything else except small personal belongings into store.

He knew that this was one of the things that he had meant to plan last night, but Olive had effectively prevented him from thinking of anything but her.

It had been after three o'clock when she had finally left him to enter her carriage, which she had told to return an hour earlier, in the charge of a sleepy coachman and a footman who was stifling a yawn as he opened the door for her.

"Do you wish me to escort you home?" Lord Alistair had enquired.

"No, of course not," Olive had replied. "I told my lady's-maid, who will tell the household, that I was visiting an aged relation who was having a small birthday-party."

Lord Alistair had laughed.

"Aged relations do not stay up so late!"

"Why should the woman question anything I do? She will be only too delighted to wait on me now that I will be a Marchioness and she will have a far better standing in the servants' hall than she has ever had before."

"Another point for the Marquis," Lord Alistair replied.

He knew it did not even anger him to hear Olive talk in

such a manner and he had finally accepted her contention that marriage was one thing and love, as far as she was concerned, was another.

When at about one o'clock Lord Alistair had found that Champkins had retired to his own bedroom, they had moved from the Sitting-Room.

As he held Olive close to him in his own comfortable bed, he had decided, now that he could think clearly, that he was glad she was not going with him to Scotland.

He was well aware how she could complain about the roughness of the sea and the lack of comfort on the ship in which they were obliged to travel.

He was also certain that while she might be impressed by the Castle, she would soon be bored to distraction, even more bored than he would be, and would not hesitate to express her feelings and doubtless show them all too clearly to his father.

He had been so concerned with his own difficulties and so confident that Olive, because she loved him, would solve them for him, that only now did he begin to see all the snags which impetuously he had ignored.

Although she was the most passionate and exciting woman he had ever known, his brain, when not befogged by desire, was aware all too clearly of her incessant craving for social power and, as her behaviour to Arina had shown, her lamentable lack of human kindness.

Only when she had left him and he had gone back to his tumbled bed, which was still redolent with the fragrance of her hair and her body, did Lord Alistair tell himself that actually he had had a very lucky escape.

No-one knew more than he did how quickly the fires of passion could die down until there was not even a smouldering ember to be ignited into flame.

'Sooner or later that will happen with Olive,' he decided.

Actually, fate had dealt him an ace when Harrowby had circumvented his plan to make Olive his wife.

"It would not have worked," he told himself in more commonplace language, when he woke the next morning.

Driving towards Bloomsbury, he thought that his new

method of avoiding his father's command was very much cleverer.

'As soon as her mother is well enough for her to return,' Lord Alistair thought, 'we will think of some plausible story which will set me free.'

What was more, his father would not live forever, and once he was the Duke, he would be able to come South as often as he liked.

He was quite certain that would mean a great number of months of the year when Scotland would have to do without him.

The sunshine seemed brighter than usual and the darkness of yesterday had passed. It seemed almost an omen of goodwill that, as he passed a newspaper-boy shouting at the corner of the street, he heard him call:

"Read of the death of two aristocrats by drowning! Read of the Duke who mourns two of his sons!"

The horses carried him away before the Marquis could hear more, but he knew it must be the report of his brothers' deaths.

He had expected that the news would make headlines in the papers, and this would mean that now all of his friends would be aware that he was the new Marquis of Kildonon.

'This is how I shall have to think of myself in the future,' he thought, and found it a far more pleasant idea than it had been the day before.

He pulled up his horses outside Number 27 and saw, as he did so, that the door of the lodging-house was open and Arina was standing in the Hall. At her feet was one small and very battered trunk.

She was wearing the same plain cotton dress and untrimmed bonnet she had worn when he had first seen her in Olive's house.

When he stepped down to take her hand in his, he saw that she had been crying. Knowing it was because she had said good-bye to her mother, he did not comment on it but merely said:

"I commend you for being the most punctual woman I

have ever known. I am glad you have not kept me waiting, as we have a great deal to do."

She gave him what he was certain was a somewhat forced smile, and having paid for her lodgings, he helped her into the Phaeton while Ben attached her small trunk to the back under the seat on which he now rode.

They set off, and the Marquis, as he was now determined to think of himself, asked:

"Your mother is all right?"

"Yes . . . thank you," Arina replied, "and the Surgeon was very pleased that she could come to him so quickly. He was . . . afraid otherwise it might be . . . too late."

Her voice trembled for a second on the last word and the Marquis knew she was fighting to appear calm and self-controlled.

"You must not forget to give me the Surgeon's address so that my secretary can send him the rest of the money."

"I have already written it down for you."

"I can see you are very punctilious, as I am," the Marquis answered. "I find it very irritating when people are careless, forgetful, and slipshod."

"I hope I shall never show any of those . . . faults while I am with . . . you."

The Marquis turned his head to smile at her and realised that despite the fact that her clothes were made of the poorest material and very unfashionable, she looked extremely neat and tidy.

She also had a little of the Spring look he had thought was especially hers when he had first seen her.

She was still pathetically thin, and he could see, as she was looking ahead to where they were going and at the horses' heads bobbing up and down, the sharpness of her chin and the hollows beneath her small cheek-bones.

'She will soon look different when she starts to eat well,' he thought to himself. 'I am sure that because she is worrying about her mother, it will take a little longer than it might do with someone else who had no such anxieties.'

As he drove back into the more popular streets, Arina asked:

"Where are we going?"

"To buy you your trousseau," the Marquis replied.

"You are aware that I shall have no . . . idea what I should . . . choose or what would be . . . correct for me to . . . wear?"

She paused before she added:

"Mama and I have always lived in the country so of course I am in fact nothing but a 'country bumpkin.' "

"That is the last thing you will look when I have finished with you," the Marquis promised. "Leave everything to me."

"I still feel very . . . embarrassed that you should not only . . . choose the right clothes for me but also . . . pay for them."

"Now you are talking like a prim and proper young lady," he replied, "and not like an actress, who would command a very large salary and exceptional benefits at Her Majesty's Theatre in the Haymarket or at Drury Lane."

Arina laughed and it was a very pretty sound.

"You can hardly expect me to aspire to anything so important as either of those Theatres."

"The Theatre in which you will act is very much more impressive, and I shall have plenty of time to tell you all about it while we are at sea."

She drew in her breath.

"Is that how we are travelling to Scotland?"

"Will it upset you?"

"I hope not. But it would be very undignified to be seasick, especially when you are present."

"Why especially me?" the Marquis enquired.

"Because you are so magnificent and I am sure you never suffer from an ordinary cold, seasickness, or tummy-pains like common people."

The Marquis laughed.

"Thank you. That is the most ingenious compliment I have ever received."

"I was only saying what I think," Arina explained. "And I did not mean it . . . rudely."

"It was not rude but delightful," he replied.

As he spoke he pulled up his horses outside a shop which was in a side-road off Bond Street. It was not large and there was nothing frightening about it.

But the Marquis was aware that Arina shrank a little in her seat and there was a worried expression in her eyes.

"Do not be afraid," he said. "I know this dressmaker well. She will be prepared to achieve miracles by providing you with everything you require in record time."

Arina did not answer, but the Marquis felt her fingers tremble in his as he helped her down from the Phaeton.

The shop was small but elegantly decorated. The woman who came towards them as they entered gave an exclamation at the sight of the Marquis and curtseyed.

"It's delightful to see you, My Lord."

Arina thought she was not only exceedingly smart in a grey dress that had an elegance about it, but she was also very attractive, despite the fact that she must be at least thirty years of age.

The Marquis had known *Madame* Celeste, as she called herself, having been born plain Cecily Brown, since he first visited the shop with the lady who had loved him so ardently that she had decorated his flat for him.

"I prefer to have original clothes," she had said, "and that is what I have found at *Madame* Celeste's."

Because after that love-affair was over Lord Alistair had taken several other beautiful women to *Madame* Celeste and advised them as to the gowns which became them most, she had been very grateful.

She had shown her gratitude by spending a quiet few days with him in a comfortable Inn in the wilds of Buckinghamshire.

Being a country girl, she was a good rider, and they had ridden over the meadowlands in the daytime and spent the nights in a low-ceilinged room with a comfortable bed filled with goose-down.

It had been an unusual delight, Lord Alistair had thought

afterwards—like picturing the simple wild-flowers of Spring, like primroses and daffodils, rather than exotic hot-house carnations and orchids.

He had helped Celeste up to the pinnacle of fame by bringing her many other clients, but this was the first time he had been in the position to buy clothes which he intended to pay for himself.

He told Celeste in a few short words exactly what he required and how quickly, and she flung up her hands in despair.

Then in the practical manner which he advised, she said:

"I will do what is possible, and the rest will have to follow wherever you may be going."

She looked at Arina and smiled.

"I think that almost everything I have at the moment will suit the lovely young lady, and for you, and you only, My Lord, I will commit the unforgivable crime of switching gowns that are nearly finished or half-finished for someone else and starting again for the original purchaser."

"That is what I expected you would say," the Marquis replied with a smile. "We shall also require shoes, underclothes, coats, capes and shawls, gloves, and all the other things which women take for granted but which mount up when you start with absolutely nothing."

Celeste gave a cry of horror.

Then she clapped her hands and ordered her assistant to bring everyone she employed from the work-rooms in the basement and the seamstresses in the attics. There were at least twenty of them.

When she told them what she required, which meant most of them having to work all night, they seemed at first interested and then delighted at the thought of the extra money they would earn.

"It'll cost you a great deal," she said in a low voice to the Marquis while she was waiting for her staff.

"It is of no consequence."

When she raised her eye-brows, he added:

"My circumstances have changed."

"I am glad, very glad, for your sake."

There was no doubt that there was sincerity in Celeste's tone, and the Marquis said:

"You have always been a very good friend, Celeste."

He looked into her eyes and saw that the affection she had had for him was still there.

Then the work-people came crowding into the small Salon and she started to tell them what was wanted.

While Arina was being measured and fitted, amazed by the thousands of different suggestions and entranced by the materials and sketches of the gowns she was shown, the Marquis went with Ben in his Phaeton to collect food.

This he knew Arina would need more urgently than he did, but he had no wish to be hungry either.

A Restaurant in Piccadilly supplied him with everything he asked for and some excellent wine, which he knew Celeste would enjoy as much as he would.

He took it back to the shop and had one of Celeste's assistants arrange it in her office, where there was just room for the three of them to sit round a small table.

Arina was looking very pale and exhausted when the Marquis returned.

But he insisted on her having half a glass of wine, which brought the colour back into her cheeks and, as he was shrewdly aware, gave her an appetite which she might otherwise not have had.

He knew that when people were near to starvation they got to a point when they no longer craved for food and actually found it extremely hard to eat.

It was then that a little wine, though certainly not too much, would stimulate the digestive juices, and once they had started to enjoy their food, it was not difficult to go on eating.

He thought too that because he and Celeste laughed and joked with each other and she teased him, Arina found it easier to relax for the moment and to forget her mother.

So brilliant was Celeste's skill and organisation that by

the time they left the shop later that afternoon, Arina was able to take with her two new trunks full of clothes and accessories, with the promise that much more would be ready the next morning before they left for Tilbury.

The remainder would follow them by sea as soon as it was possible to get it completed.

Celeste had sent one of her more intelligent employees to buy Arina the slippers she needed and, on the Marquis's suggestion, a pair of stouter shoes for walking on the moors.

"Will I really be able to do that?" Arina asked.

"If you want to."

"Of course I will want to," she replied.

He was surprised, then thought it was something he might have expected in a girl who had always lived in the country.

He therefore increased the order to two pairs of shoes and suggested that Celeste make her a gown that was not too long, in which it would be easy to walk.

"She cannot be so immodest as to show her ankles, My Lord," Celeste teased.

"But it must certainly not be so long that she trips over it," the Marquis retorted.

Arina gave a little laugh.

"I am glad you did not see me in the countryside where we lived with Papa."

The Marquis did not answer, he only thought that what Miss Arina Beverley could do was very different and would not be tolerated in the presumed Marchioness of Kildonon.

They drove back to the flat.

Now the Marquis remembered that he had to tell Champkins he was married. He was quite sure that his valet would find it hard to believe, but it was essential that if Champkins was suspicious that the marriage was a pretence, he should not voice such ideas in Scotland.

He played with the thought of not taking Champkins with him, but decided it would be intolerable never to have anything but Scottish servants around him.

They would not be trained to the quiet, perfect service

that he had found in his grandfather's house or in the great houses of the families whom he had visited without his own valet.

When he helped Arina down from the Phaeton outside his flat in Half-Moon Street, he thought she looked very different from the girl he had picked up at Bloomsbury earlier in the day.

The fashionable pale blue muslin she wore had French ribbons of the same colour crossing her chest and passing under her small breasts, to tie in a sash at her back.

All the gowns the Marquis had bought for her were very high-waisted, as was the fashion which had just arrived from France and which had been set by Josephine Bonaparte, wife of the First Consul.

Over her gown Arina wore a silk shawl patterned in blue, and her bonnet with its fashionably high crown and tipped-up brim was decorated with wild-flowers and tied under her chin with blue ribbon.

It made her look very young and at the same time, the Marquis thought, lovely, despite the fact that she was undoubtedly tired and far too thin.

They went upstairs, and having taken her into the Sitting-Room the Marquis went in search of Champkins, whom he found, as he had expected, still packing but now not in trunks but in wooden cases which were arranged on the floor above.

"I didn't hear you come in, M'Lord," Champkins exclaimed, getting to his feet.

"I have something to tell you."

"Yes, M'Lord?"

"When we leave for Scotland tomorrow morning you and I are taking my wife with us."

Champkins opened his eyes wide and exclaimed:

"Blimey, that's a surprise!"

The Marquis laughed because he could not help it.

"I think it will also be a surprise to quite a number of people in the North. There are reasons, Champkins, for my having such a precipitate marriage, but what is impor-

tant is that everyone in Scotland must believe it happened
at least two months ago."

It was typical of the man, the Marquis thought, that
without asking any questions Champkins merely said:

"If that's what you tells I, M'Lord, that's what I believes."

"Thank you, Champkins. I have already told Mr. Faulkner, as I have told His Grace, that the reason for my
marriage being kept secret is that my wife is in mourning
for her father."

As he spoke the Marquis suddenly remembered it was
something he had not told Celeste and therefore Arina's
clothes were in every colour of the rainbow. There was no
black amongst them.

Quickly, so that he hoped that even Champkins would
be deceived, he added:

"Her Ladyship is, however, not wearing black because
it was her father's express instruction that no-one should
mourn for him. He was, I believe, almost fanatical on the
subject and she must naturally obey his wishes. Although
deeply distressed at losing him, she wears the gowns she
has always worn in the colours that pleased him when he
was alive."

"Very sensible, if I may say so, M'Lord," Champkins
remarked. "I always thought all that weeping and wailing
were nothing more than eye-wash."

"I agree with you," the Marquis said.

Having told Champkins to inform the Chef, when he
came in, that there would be two for dinner, he hurried
away to warn Arina about the explanation he had just
invented.

"It was very stupid of me," he confessed. "I should in
fact have dressed you in black, mauve, white, and perhaps
gray."

Arina smiled.

She had taken off her bonnet while he was upstairs, and
now in her blue dress, her hair arranged by Celeste in a
new style, she looked very elegant and very pretty.

"I have been looking at myself in the mirror," she said.
"This is by far the loveliest gown I have ever had! And I

am so thrilled with the ones that are in pink and green that I could not bear to lose them."

"We will just have to stick to our story that your father disliked mourning."

"It is actually true," Arina replied. "He used to say that it was nonsense that people gave so many flowers when someone died and had never thought to take them a bouquet when they were alive."

Then she added:

"When Papa died, Mama and I could not afford new clothes, so we just trimmed those we had with black ribbon."

"You reassure me that I am not telling a lie," the Marquis said. "It is something I hate doing, and I am sure you do too, so we shall tell as few people as possible. But those which have to pass our lips are of course white lies and therefore are not reprehensible."

He was surprised when Arina, giving a little laugh, asked:

"Are you placating your own conscience or mine?"

Because she had been so quiet and frightened ever since he had known her, he liked the sudden sparkle that seemed to be in her eyes, and he said:

"I think if we are clever we might have quite a lot of fun out of this adventure, which is the way we must think of it."

"Yes, of course. And it is exciting to go adventuring now, after being so worried about Mama, so frightened I would never find the money for her operation."

"You are not to think about it anymore," the Marquis said firmly. "I have not asked you before, but when is your mother going to have her operation?"

"In three days' time," Arina answered. "The Surgeon, who is a very kind man, wants not only first to feed her properly but to give her certain medicines which will make her feel stronger."

When she spoke Arina clasped her hands together, and then she said in a voice that was very moving:

"I am praying, praying all the time that it will be a success. If it is, it will be entirely due to you. I can never, never . . . tell you . . . how grateful I am or how . . . wonderful I think . . . you are."

Chapter Five

Because Arina's clothes were packed for travelling the Marquis suggested that they should not change for dinner, which meant that he would not have to change either.

This was a blessing, as he had not yet decided how he should sort out their sleeping arrangements.

They ate a delicious dinner in the small Dining-Room and Arina enjoyed every mouthful she could manage.

All too soon she said with a little sigh:

"I cannot eat any more, but I cannot bear to think of wasting this marvellous food."

"I do not think it will be wasted," the Marquis replied. "At the same time, in Scotland they will be astonished if you do not manage a large breakfast, a large luncheon, and an even larger tea, followed of course by an enormous evening-meal!"

Arina gave a cry of horror and then said, a sparkle in her eyes:

"If I grow fat on so much food you will find it very expensive."

The Marquis laughed.

"Perhaps my money will be expended in a good cause, but I doubt if you will ever be one of the 'fat kine'."

"I hope not," Arina replied. "But I know it shocks you

how thin I am now, and *Madame* Celeste was horrified at how my bones stuck through my skin."

It struck the Marquis that although she might be too thin she would be very attractive without any clothes on at all.

Then he told himself that he had no intention of thinking of her as a woman and that he must be very careful not to shock her, since otherwise she would not trust him in the way she did now.

He was experienced enough to know that the way Arina looked at him and what she said about his saving her mother's life were simply the reactions of a child who had been rescued from danger by somebody she not only trusted but respected.

It made him feel old, but he told himself that was what he was in Arina's eyes.

At the same time, from his point of view he knew it was a relief that he was not taking Olive with him to Scotland.

Arina might be afraid that she would shame him or let him down, but Olive's looks and behaviour would undoubtedly have proved an embarrassment.

The Scots would never have understood and would have branded her as a scarlet woman immediately they saw her.

Because he had been convinced that she alone could save him from having to marry the woman of his father's choice, he had not considered until now her impact on the Clan.

Her crimson lips and mascaraed eye-lashes, now that he thought about it, and her rouged cheeks, while the vogue in London, would have horrified the Scots and made them sure that she was a harlot.

'This is exactly what she is!' the Marquis thought with a cynical twist to his lips, 'and Harrowby is welcome to her!'

When he thought of the way she had behaved last night, he knew he had had a very lucky escape and that Olive would be unfaithful both to her husband and to her lovers.

In fact, she was really the last type of woman he desired as his wife.

He thought that nevertheless he would miss her, but not for very long.

None of his love-affairs had ever lasted for any length of time, and as soon as the fires of passion had died down he forgot the woman in question and was ready for somebody new to attract him.

Then the whole game started all over again.

When they had finished dinner the Marquis took Arina into the Sitting-Room and produced the contract he had made out.

She scanned it carefully, reading every word. It stated that he had employed her for the sum of five hundred pounds to act temporarily the part of his wife. When their association was over, she would make no claims on him, but would disappear out of his life and not communicate with him again, unless he desired it.

Finally she read:

When we say good-bye, I promise to pay annually the sum of two hundred pounds in half-yearly instalments into Miss Beverley's Bank.

It was all very clear and concise. When she had finished reading what he had written, Arina said:

"There is no necessity for you to give me so much money after I have left you. I have already said that when Mama is quite well again, I will find some work to do."

"What sort of work?" the Marquis enquired.

"I am not certain," Arina replied, "but I thought I might be able to copy some of the beautiful nightgowns you bought for me yesterday and the . . . other things as well."

She looked away from him and the Marquis knew she thought it immodest to mention the chemises he had given her, which were lace-trimmed and delicately stitched.

"I think you would find that rather hard work and without the security of knowing that you have a regular amount of money coming in," he remarked. "But of course, Arina, as I have said before, sooner or later you will be married properly to somebody who will take care of you and who will also be prepared to provide for your mother."

There was silence for a moment as she thought over what he had said. Then she answered:

"Because you are so kind and thoughtful, may I accept your proposition for the moment with the promise that if I have no . . . further need of your money in the future I can write to you and . . . say so?"

"Of course," the Marquis agreed.

"Shall I sign this document?"

In answer he handed her the big white quill-pen, dipping it first into an ornate gold ink-well.

Her writing was neat and tidy, and when he too had signed the paper the Marquis folded it and said:

"I intend to send this to my Bank. It will be safe there and no prying eyes will see it. At the same time, I will instruct them to pay the rest of the money which is owed to your mother's Surgeon, and three hundred pounds into your Bank, if you will tell me where it is."

Arina hesitated and he said:

"On second thought, I think perhaps it would be a mistake to use a Bank where you are known and which would be aware that you are receiving money from me. It would be better if I open an account in your name at Coutt's and you can draw the money from there whenever you require it."

"Thank you very much," Arina answered. "I am sure what you have thought of is best for both of us."

The Marquis thought she was being very amenable, and because he was sure it would please her, he said:

"I want you now to sit down comfortably while I tell you things about my family which you will be expected to know when you arrive in Scotland. I will also describe my father, whom I suspect you will find as intimidating as I have always done."

Arina crossed the Sitting-Room to settle herself in a large, comfortable armchair in front of the fireplace.

As if he felt restless, the Marquis did not sit down but instead walked about as he started what was really the story of his life.

"My father was brought up by his father to think the

world was there for him to walk on," he began. "Most Scottish Chieftains are the same. For centuries they have enjoyed power, and although ostensibly it was taken from them by the British, in the heart of their own Clan they still reign supreme."

He paused for a moment, thinking that was particularly true of his father. Then he went on:

"When my father inherited, he was the most important Chieftain in Scotland, besides being the richest and the greatest land-owner."

"I have heard of him and of your Castle," Arina murmured.

The Marquis was surprised, but he did not say so and continued:

"He revived the old customs, the old ceremonies, and the mystique which surrounded the Chieftains of the Clans. As soon as the ban was lifted on the wearing of the tartan, he put his own servants and all the Clansmen in the vicinity of the Castle into the kilt."

As he spoke the Marquis was thinking of how bitterly the Scots had resented having to give up the clothes that in many ways were a part of their faith.

Because it meant so much to them, they had dipped the traditional cloth of the tartan in vats of mud or dye and sewed the cloth into ludicrous breeches.

In this way they felt that somehow they deceived the British and made the new laws seem foolish.

At first, when the ban on Highland dress was lifted in 1782, it became an affectation of the Anglicised Lairds, the fancy-dress of the Lowlanders, and the uniform of the King's Gaelic soldiers.

But eventually a great number of Clans followed the McDonons, and now more and more Highlanders were looking proud and resplendent in the kilt and the plaid.

The Marquis tried to put this into words so that Arina would understand a little about the land to which he was taking her.

But even as he spoke he knew in reality how little he

knew about the Highlands himself, having been away from them for so long.

He suddenly felt absurdly angry that at the age of nearly twenty-seven he should be forced to return like a captured slave to face his father's overbearing domination, which would gradually wear him down until he would surrender not only himself but his independence of thought.

"When you get to Kildonon Castle," he said aloud, "and realise that the whole world revolves in accordance with my father's whim, that even the sun shines and the tides go in and out at his command, you will understand what the place is like far better than I can tell you now."

Only as he finished speaking the words that seemed to ring out because they were spoken with anger and hatred did he realise that Arina was asleep.

Intent on his own thoughts, he had not noticed that she had not interrupted him or asked any questions for a long time.

Now, as he saw that her eyes were closed, he knew she was utterly and completely exhausted by all she had been through.

The emotion of leaving her mother at the Nursing-home had been followed by the long hours of standing as gown after gown was tried on her.

Then had come the ordeal of driving away alone with him.

Perhaps it was his Celt ancestry which had made him aware that she was embarrassed and apprehensive when he had drawn his horses to a standstill outside the building in which his flat was situated.

He had known too that while they had dinner together she was nervous at first and afraid of doing or saying anything of which he would not approve.

When he thought about it, he was sure that it was the first time she had ever dined alone with a man. Perhaps he should have been more understanding and more gentle with her, but he was not quite certain how to do so.

The women with whom he dined alone always made sure that the conversation sparkled with *double extendres* and looked at him in a way which was an incitement to passion.

In fact, the Marquis could not remember when he had had a meal alone with a woman who was not intent on arousing his desire and making herself indispensable to him.

'Arina is only a child,' he thought. 'I shall not only have to teach her what she must do, but protect her from the things that frighten her, and undoubtedly there will be a great many of them.'

Looking down at her as she lay asleep with her head turned against the softness of the silk cushion, she looked very young and very vulnerable.

He saw too that her eye-lashes, which had seemed dark against her pale skin, wore no mascara like Olive's, but were naturally dark but turned to gold as they curled at the tips.

They were in fact the eye-lashes of a very young child, and the Marquis felt that she was not only young and fragile, but like an exquisite piece of Dresden china that might easily be broken if handled roughly.

He opened the door, then picked her up in his arms to carry her to his bedroom.

He had vaguely been wondering how they could sleep apart without Champkins being aware of it, and he knew now that because Arina was asleep there would be no need to involve her in any conspiracy.

He laid her down carefully on the bed that had been turned down for the night.

He thought he should wake her so that she could undress and get into bed, then realised she was so deeply asleep that it would be almost cruel to do so.

Instead he took off her shoes, then skilfully unbuttoned her gown and slipped it off.

He thought with a wry smile that it was the first time he had undressed a woman who was not in the least interested in what he was doing.

He slipped her between the sheets and saw what she had meant when she said that *Madame* Celeste had been shocked at how thin she was. She was indeed far too light for her age and height.

He pulled the bed-clothes up to her chin, and by the rise and fall of her breasts he knew she was so deeply asleep that it would take a great deal more than his gentle movements to wake her.

He stood looking down at her. Then he took one of the pillows from the bed and picked up his night-shirt and robe from the chair on which Champkins had laid them ready for him.

Going to the cupboard, he found, as he expected, two blankets folded and ready in case he should need their extra warmth.

Carrying them all in his arms, he blew out the candles beside the bed, then left the room, closing the door behind him.

The sofa in the Sitting-Room was large and comfortable, and because he too was tired, as thanks to Olive he had slept very little the night before, the Marquis expected to fall asleep immediately, but it was nearly midnight before he did so.

Having been in the Army for two years after leaving Oxford, he had taught himself to wake at any time he wished without the need of being called.

It was something which he had found useful in his Regimental life and later, when, for instance, he wished to go cubbing on his grandfather's Estate, which involved getting up at four o'clock when the servants sometimes overslept.

The Marquis was therefore bathed and half-dressed before Champkins came down from his room on the next floor.

"Good-morning, M'Lord!" he exclaimed. "You're early!"

"I have a few things to tidy up before we leave," the Marquis said, "and as Her Ladyship is still asleep, I had no wish to wake her."

Champkins glanced towards the closed bedroom door.

"Very wise, M'Lord, if I may say so. Her Ladyship may find it hard to sleep when she's tossed about on the waves."

"I hope the sea will be calm at this time of the year," the Marquis replied drily. "And now, Champkins, I want to make sure we have everything with us that is of importance, because I am giving Mr. Groves instructions that everything else must go into store."

Mr. Groves was the secretary, who was expected to arrive at nine o'clock.

Champkins made a grimace.

"Does that mean, M'Lord, that we're not coming back?"

"If we do, it will not be to this flat, but to Kildonon House in Park Lane," the Marquis said in a hard voice.

He spoke with a determination that made Champkins look at him in surprise.

He had suddenly made up his mind that he would fight his father in this matter if in nothing else and would refuse to make his home in Scotland unless he had what at any rate would be a *pied à terre* in London.

He thought perhaps it was the way he had explained things to Arina last night—of which she had heard very little—which had given him a new courage that he should not have lost in the first place.

It was almost as if in telling her about the Scots and how despite the overbearing and cruel domination by the English they had kept their identity and their pride, he had found both those things within himself.

"In fact," he said now, "why should we pay for storage when there is plenty of room at Kildonon House? There will be a caretaker there, and I will tell Mr. Groves to have everything removed from here and placed in the Ball-Room until I can arrange them as I wish."

"A good idea, M'Lord," Champkins said cheerfully, but the Marquis was not listening.

* * *

When Mr. Faulkner arrived he brought two large carriages which were more comfortable than hackney-carriages and which were drawn by two strong horses.

The Marquis, Arina, and Mr. Faulkner were to travel in

the first, and Champkins in the second with all the baggage.

By the time they left, two more trunks had arrived for Arina from *Madame* Celeste, along with three leather hat-boxes containing the bonnets to match the clothes they had ordered.

"What we have to decide," the Marquis said with a smile at the mountain of luggage, "is what you will need on the voyage and what must go down into the hold. I doubt if any cabin, however large, could accommodate all this."

Because Arina could only look helplessly at her new pile of possessions, the Marquis was relieved to discover that Celeste, with her usual common sense, had itemised the contents of each trunk.

He therefore chose the one which he thought would be most useful, then opened another to take from it a long, warm cape which was trimmed with fur.

"It can be very cold at sea," he explained as Arina looked at it in surprise.

Champkins had seen to his luggage and the Marquis had contributed at the last moment a certain amount of food from Shepherd Market and also a few cases of wine.

There was a trunk containing what the Marquis knew was essential on a journey of this sort—his own linen sheets, towels, and blankets, besides soft pillows and bedside rugs.

It rather amused him that Arina was astonished that they should travel in such luxury.

But when she saw her cabin aboard The *Sea Serpent*, which was the ship that sailed regularly from Tilbury to Aberdeen, she understood how the Marquis found its inadequate furnishings extremely uncomfortable.

However, for her it was very exciting not only to be at sea in what seemed a large ship but also to have a cabin to herself.

Because they had been so poor after her father's death, she and her mother when they moved into a tiny cottage had been forced to share a bedroom.

Staying in London, they could hardly afford the cheapest room in a boarding-house, let alone pay for two.

When Champkins had made up Arina's bunk with linen sheets that were too big for it, fluffy white blankets, and comfortable pillows, she thanked him so effusively that he said:

"It's your right, M'Lady, now that you're married to the Master, an' if you'll take my advice you should always see that you has what you're entitled to."

"The difficulty is," Arina replied, "I am not at all certain what that means."

She spoke spontaneously and frankly to Champkins because she already liked him and realised how devoted he was to the Marquis.

In fact, she thought of Champkins as being very like the Nanny she had had until her parents became too poor to afford one and she was old enough to look after herself.

Champkins grinned. Then he said:

"What you have to do, M'Lady, is to stick yer nose in the air, and look down at everybody else as if you was superior to 'em!"

Arina laughed.

"I am quite certain I shall never feel superior to anybody!"

"Just you remember Your Ladyship's as good as what they are, if not better!"

Arina laughed again, and she felt as if Champkins took away some of the apprehension she felt in case she should do something wrong and fail the Marquis by making his relatives suspicious that their marriage was not real.

'He has been so kind to me that it would be unforgivable if I could not help him,' she thought

She had felt very shy when she had awakened in the morning to find herself in what she knew was the Marquis's bed, and was aware who had put her there and removed her gown.

At first she was so horrified at the thought of what had occurred that she had wanted to run away and hide and never see the Marquis again.

Then she told herself she was being ridiculous.

After all, she was of no importance in his eyes, and it was a very sensible thing to do to take off the expensive gown he had given her, which would certainly have been very creased if she had slept in it all night.

He would have done the same for any woman, old or young, she thought.

She decided that if she appeared shy, embarrassed, or coy about the situation she had caused by going to sleep, it would make her look foolish and the Marquis would doubtless despise her.

Arina wondered how he knew how to remove her gown and undo the buttons at the back of it.

Then, when she had arranged her hair at the dressing-table, she found something which was very surprising.

It was a very masculine dressing-table, very much the same as the one her father had used, but much more luxurious.

The Marquis's brushes, which were of ivory engraved with his crest, stood on top of the low chest-of-drawers on which there was a mirror supported in a way that it could be adjusted to any angle.

Framed in wood, it had three little drawers beneath it.

Arina found it fascinating, and because it was like her father's, without thinking or meaning to pry, she opened the middle drawer.

Inside were a number of loose coins and on top of them a small swan's-down powder-puff.

What she could not have known was that Olive had dropped it by mistake after she had dressed herself the night before and stood in front of the mirror to arrange her hair and repair the ravages of the Marquis's kisses.

She had also powdered her nose, and when she had taken a small box of salve from her reticule to redden her lips, the powder-puff had fallen onto the floor, where Champkins had found it.

It had not surprised him.

It was only another of the things which his Master's "love-birds," as he called them in his mind, left behind. Hair-pins, lip-salves, small bottles of perfume, and even at

times articles of clothing, had all been retrieved by
Champkins without comment.

He had pushed the powder-puff into the drawer, meaning
to mention it to the Marquis later.

Arina stared at it with puzzled eyes.

Then she told herself she was being stupid.

Of course the Marquis, seeing how attractive he was,
would have had many women in his life!

Although she was slightly shocked that they should
have come to what she realised was a bachelor's flat, she
supposed that they had as good an excuse as she had for
being there.

Anyway, she told herself, it was none of her business.

However, because for the first time she thought of the
Marquis as a man rather than an angel sent from God to
save her mother from dying, she could not help being
curious.

When she went into the Dining-Room for breakfast she
had longed to ask him if he had slept comfortably after
giving up his bedroom to her, but she found it impossible
to express what she wanted to say.

Instead, she tried to speak to him quite naturally, and
not to remember that he had undressed her and put her to
bed.

As it happened, the Marquis was so busy with his
preparations for leaving that he had almost forgotten what
had happened the night before.

Mr. Groves had arrived while they were still having
breakfast, and by the time he had been given his instructions, Mr. Faulkner was announced.

All Arina had to do was put on her bonnet and the blue
shawl she had worn the day before, and climb into the
carriage.

As they drove away from London, her thoughts were
only with her mother, and she was praying that she would
already be feeling stronger so that there would be less risk
when she was ready for her operation.

She had told her mother why she was going away and

had promised to write to her every day, although she was not quite certain whether she understood.

"I shall have plenty of time on board ship," she told herself.

The only thing she had asked Champkins to put into a valise was writing-paper.

"I can do better for you than that, M'Lady," Champkins had replied.

Arina had not asked him what he meant at the time, but before he made up the bunk in her cabin, he put a fine leather blotter down on the table and set beside it a small travelling ink-pot and several quill-pens.

"I'll keep them sharpened for you, M'Lady," he promised, and Arina found it hard to tell him how grateful she was.

Only when the ship was actually moving out of the harbour did she feel a sudden tremble of fear at the thought of leaving her mother and everything that was familiar.

She was going to a strange place with a strange man to be with people who, from all she had heard, sounded very frightening—the Duke in particular.

Then she told herself that, as the Marquis had said, it was an adventure, and she would be extremely ungrateful and very foolish if she did not make every effort to enjoy it.

She knew it was something her mother would have felt before she had become so ill.

Her father too had always seemed to make everything they did not only an excitement but also a joyous experience which they would remember and talk about.

Perhaps because he had given up so much when he ran away with her mother, Arina felt he used his imagination as few other grown-up people bothered to do.

It was not only the tales he had told her when she was a little girl of fairies and goblins in the woods, of dragons that lived in the forests, and of nymphs that inhabited the streams.

It was also that his imagination enabled him to live in an enchanted world where stark reality never encroached.

When he told his wife that he loved her and it was difficult to think of anyone else, he spoke the truth. And because she looked at him with starry eyes, their marriage had been an idyllic one.

That they lived in a shabby, dilapidated house and could not afford any luxuries was of no importance!

To them it was a Fairy-Palace; the food they ate was enchanted, and their daughter was not only a gift from God but a fairy-child, looked after and protected by the fairies.

Only after her father had died did she and her mother have to face reality, and it was very frightening.

Arina knew now that her fears were groundless, because her father was still loving and protecting them, wherever he might be now, and had sent the Marquis to rescue them.

She chided herself for ever thinking that they had been forsaken.

"This is a ship like the one in which Odysseus sailed away from Troy or Jason sought the Golden Fleece," she thought as the *Sea Serpent* began to move over the waves, "and the Marquis is a Knight with a sword in his hand, a shield on his arm, ready to destroy any enemies or dragons that may assail us."

She looked up at the sky as she said beneath her breath:

"Wherever we go, whatever we do, we are protected, and I have only to pray to Papa for help for my prayers to be answered."

She smiled as she asked herself:

"How can I have been so foolish as not to have known this before now? It was wrong, very wrong of me to let Mama be so unhappy and grow so ill because she felt we had been forsaken."

She wished she could tell her mother what she had discovered, then she knew she could write it to her. It might be hard to put into words, but her mother would understand.

What she had reasoned out for herself made her feel so happy that when Champkins came to tell her that the

Marquis had arranged for them to have something to eat,
she went to him with a smile on her lips, her eyes alight
with happiness.

It was after one o'clock when they sailed, and because
there were no other passangers aboard the *Sea Serpent*,
Mr. Faulkner had been able to engage a third cabin,
where they could eat on their own.

It was impossible to move the bunks because they were
battened down, but all the rest of the furniture had been
removed except for a small round table, three chairs, and
a side-table from which food could be served.

A steward waited on them, and Arina realised as soon as
a rich pâté was offered her that this was the food the
Marquis had brought with him.

The pâté was followed by an ox-tongue, well cooked and
set in aspic. There was also a salad and a whole leg of pork
garnished with apples, if Arina preferred it.

The Marquis was hungry and ate quite a lot of what he
referred to as a "light luncheon."

With difficulty Arina prevented herself from commenting
that so much food would have sufficed her and her mother
for weeks.

She almost felt as if Champkins were beside her, telling
her that she must behave as if such a meal were quite
ordinary, and far from being impressed by it, she should
feel entitled to complain.

Then she gave a little chuckle at her thoughts and the
Marquis looked up to ask:

"What is amusing you?"

"Something Champkins said."

"He is certainly a character," the Marquis remarked,
"and I am wondering how he will get on at the Castle.
With any other man I would be afraid that he might be
bullied for being a Sassenach, but I have a feeling that
Champkins will hold his own."

"I am sure he will, My Lord," Mr. Faulkner agreed,
"and I assure you, we are not such barbarians as you are
making us out to be."

The Marquis laughed. Then he said:

"If you are going to be touchy about what I say, I promise you, I shall turn round and go straight back to London. I am well aware that my father will disapprove of my appearance, my conversation, and undoubtedly my thoughts, but he will have to take me as I am, or rather what I have become, living in the South!"

Mr. Faulkner did not reply, but Arina thought she had been right in thinking that the Marquis was a Knight in armour, ready to do battle with whoever opposed him.

The sea was a little choppy but not rough, and Arina stood on deck for a long time after luncheon, watching the coast of England in the distance and looking across the North Sea to where the sky met the waves.

"You look as if you are enjoying yourself," the Marquis said with just a hint of envy in his voice.

"I have suddenly realised how exciting this all is," Arina replied, "and you were right when you said it was an adventure."

"Not a very pleasant one for me."

"But it must be!" Arina insisted. "Adventures even if they are dangerous and uncomfortable are still stimulating, and I am quite certain they open new horizons which we never knew existed before."

She spoke in a rapt little voice that made the Marquis look at her in surprise.

He had expected her to be apprehensive and embarrassed! Instead, he thought, she seemed to glow almost as if she were lit from a light within and to be vibrating to it.

"I am glad you think like that," he said. "I was afraid you would be so unhappy at leaving your mother, as I know you were yesterday morning, that we were in for a very gloomy voyage."

"It would be very selfish of me if I thought only of myself," Arina replied, "and I have read that Knights when they set out to vanquish evil were always inspired by the lady whose favour they carried."

She paused and then said a little shyly:

"As I am the only . . . lady with you at the moment, I am hoping that perhaps in a very . . . small way I can . . . inspire you or at least . . . prevent you from feeling . . . resentful."

She hesitated over the word and the Marquis asked:

"How are you aware that that is what I feel? I do not remember saying so in so many words."

"You may think it very impertinent of me," Arina replied looking away from him, "but when you told me you did not wish to return to Scotland and your father was forcing you to marry a Scottish girl, I could feel how deeply it . . . angered you and how you hated and . . . resented leaving London and all your . . . friends."

As she said the word "friends" she remembered the powder-puff by the mirror on his dressing-table, and thought perhaps that was another reason why the Marquis had no wish to go away.

"What you felt is indeed true," he answered. "I think it was very perceptive of you to be aware of it, and I am sure that you will be able to help me."

"I hope so," Arina said, "but I have not yet been able to tell you how . . . ashamed I am that I fell asleep when you were telling me such interesting things last night."

She looked up at him and added beseechingly:

"Please . . . please . . . do not be offended, but tell me again what you were saying then, and I . . . promise I will not go to . . . sleep."

The Marquis smiled.

"It was understandable. You had had a very long day, and I suspect you had not slept very much the night before."

Arina knew this was true not only because she had been worried at the thought of leaving her mother, but also because her mother needed so much attention. She had risen half-a-dozen times during the hours of darkness to smooth her pillows or give her something to drink.

"It was still very rude of me," she said. "You know if I could help you in any way . . . it would be the most . . . wonderful thing that could ever happen, and it is in fact only if I can do . . . something for you that I shall ever feel out of your . . . debt."

"I have already explained that I am in *your* debt," the Marquis replied, "so I will certainly continue the story I started last night. I think you are intelligent enough to realise that, if we were actually man and wife, you would know a great deal more about me than you know now."

"I would like that . . . I would like it . . . very much."

"Very well," the Marquis agreed, "but as you are tired and beginning to feel a little cold from the wind which is filling the sails, we will go below for your first lesson."

"I have a great deal to learn," Arina admitted, "and it will be very exciting for me . . . but I only hope it will not . . . bore you."

Because she was so eager to help the Marquis, when Champkins came to her cabin to enquire if there was anything she wanted from her trunks which he had not unpacked already, she said to him:

"I . . . I want to ask you something."

"What is it, M'Lady?"

"Because this is all very new to me, if you can think of anything I can do to help His Lordship and make him feel happier, will you be frank and tell me?"

Champkins looked at her for a moment in surprise. Then he said:

"I don't mind telling you, M'Lady, that it took me by surprise when the Master tells me he's married. But now I've seen you, and when Your Ladyship says things like that to me, I thinks that you're just the sort of person who should be with him at this moment."

"Why this moment?" Arina asked.

"Because he's browned off, fed up, and sick of the whole thing," Champkins answered. "He got away from them stuck-up Scots once, and now he's got to go back again, and there's nothing he can do about it."

Arina looked at him wide-eyed.

"I know that because his brothers have died, he is now the Marquis and will one day be Chief of the Clan," she said, "but does he have to go back even if he does not wish to?"

"He's got no choice," Champkins answered. "He's got

to go back and get used to stuffing himself with haggis, or whatever it is them Scots stuff themselves with, and enjoy it!"

He did not add that he had heard this by listening at the door when Mr. Faulkner had been telling his Master that he had to return to Scotland.

He had expected it anyway, which was why he had not protested when the Marquis had said they were leaving immediately for Kildonon Castle.

"It will be difficult for him to adjust himself," Arina said as if she was speaking her thoughts aloud.

" 'Course it will, M'Lady," Champkins agreed. "What else do you think it would be, giving up his friends, his Clubs, and his lady-loves?"

The last words came out before he could prevent them. Then he said quickly:

" 'Scuse me, M'Lady, I shouldn't have said that."

"Why not, when we are speaking frankly?" Arina replied. "Of course I suspected that His Lordship, because he is so handsome, would have lots of lovely ladies in . . . love with him."

"Dozens of 'em!" Champkins said with relish. "They flutters round him like moths round a flame. But he soon gets bored with 'em. Then they comes crying to me: 'When can I see him, Champkins?' 'Please, Champkins, put this note where he can't miss it!' "

Champkins spoke in a mimicking, affected manner which made Arina want to laugh. Then he went on:

"They tips me, an' they tips me well, M'Lady, but there's nothing I can do. Once the Master's bored, he's bored! And your Ladyship can guess as soon as one lady goes out another comes in, just waiting for the opportunity."

"If they are beautiful, why does he grow . . . bored so quickly?" Arina asked.

Champkins scratched his head.

"Can't rightly say, M'Lady. Some of 'em are so beautiful you'd think that would be sufficient for any man. But if you asks me, I think it's 'cause they gets too demanding, they wants too much, and no man likes to think he's shackled to a gold-digger."

There was a humour in his voice that once again made Arina want to laugh.

"Oh, Champkins, you are so funny!" she said. "But I know exactly what you mean."

While she could understand the Marquis's desire for freedom, she thought that her father had been "shackled" to her mother, as he would have put it, and yet they had been blissfully happy for nearly nineteen years.

Then she wondered if theirs was the sort of love the Marquis was looking for, and when he did not find it he grew bored.

Perhaps he was different from her father, but they were both exceedingly handsome, both educated in the same way, and both had been brought up in luxury.

The only difference was that while her father had given up everything for love, the Marquis had been prepared to sacrifice nothing, and that probably meant that he had never loved in the same way as her father had.

'But perhaps he is seeking it,' Arina thought, 'and that will be a quest in which I can help him.'

She was not certain how, but she thought that if he could find the type of love that had made her father so happy, then she would, as she had said to him, be able to feel that she had paid her debt.

"I will pray for him," she decided, "and perhaps Papa will help him just as he helped Mama and me."

Champkins unpacked a very pretty gown of pale green gauze which had a velvet cape edged with maribou to wear over it.

When Arina had dressed herself, she wished there were a large mirror in which she could see her reflection, knowing that the gown was the loveliest she could possibly imagine.

She knew it eclipsed the blue one which she had thought when she put it on must have been fashioned from a piece of the sky.

She found attached to the gown a matching ribbon, the

same which decorated the bodice, and which *Madame* Celeste had shown her how to wear in her hair.

"If you have jewels or combs you will not need it," she had said, "but if not, you will find it very effective."

Jewels were something that she was never likely to possess, Arina thought, as she tied the ribbon in her hair with a little bow on the top.

It gave her a mischievous look which was different from the way she had looked before.

She knew also that because the green of the gown reflected the green of her eyes, it made her skin seem very white in contrast.

The evening was warm and delightful as she walked to the cabin where they were to dine.

When she entered it she found the Marquis was waiting for her, and she realised as she glanced at the table that it was laid for only two people.

She felt her heart leap because they were to be alone, and it would certainly more exciting than if Mr. Faulkner were there.

As if the Marquis knew what she was thinking, he said:

"Faulkner asked to be excused, partly, I think, through tact, and partly because he says he is tired and wishes to retire to his cabin to have a long night's rest."

"I suppose it is rude to say that I am glad," Arina replied, "but I would rather be alone with you, because that makes it so much easier to talk, and perhaps you could go on teaching me."

The Marquis thought that most women wanted to be alone with him for a very different reason.

"I do not want you to become bored with me," he teased.

"I could never be that," Arina answered, "and I promise you that even if I am, I will not fall asleep!"

She paused before she added:

"What I am afraid of is that *you* will grow bored with teaching me."

The way she accentuated the word "you" made the Marquis look at her sharply.

"As you can imagine," he began, "when . . ."

Then he stopped and changed what he had been about to say.

"You have been talking to Champkins."

Arina blushed.

"How did you know?"

"Shall I say I can read your thoughts, and I have a very good idea what Champkins would tell you, which of course is that I am easily bored."

"I am sure it is because you are so . . . intelligent that most people must find it very hard to . . . keep up with you."

Arina thought she had been ingenious in her answer, and the Marquis said with a smile:

"You are not to believe everything that Champkins tells you. He has been with me for so many years that he is inclined to become somewhat familiar."

"I feel he is very much like my Nanny. She was always telling me things 'for my own good'!"

The Marquis laughed.

"I have often thought that myself, and if Champkins were a woman he would undoubtedly be a Nanny who would rule children with a rod of iron one minute, and spoil them the next."

"That is a wonderful description of him, and I think he is a very nice man!"

They talked animatedly while they were served a delicious meal which the Marquis had brought aboard with him, and there was also champagne, which Arina had tasted before but only on very special occasions.

"Papa used to open a bottle at Christmas and on Mama's birthday," she said. "I was allowed a sip when I was small, and half a glassful when I was a little older."

"Now that you are a grown-up young lady, and of course a Marchioness," the Marquis said, "I think you can manage nearly a full glass."

"Suppose I grow unsteady on my feet?"

"Then I will carry you to bed as I did last night."

She blushed as she remembered how he had undressed her, and he thought she looked very attractive.

Then she said in a serious little voice:

"It was . . . very kind of you . . . and I did not thank you this morning because I felt it was . . . something you had already . . . forgotten."

The Marquis looked puzzled.

"Why should you think that?"

"Because I am of no . . . importance, and therefore you would not . . . remember me as you would . . ."

She stopped as if she felt that what she had begun to say was embarrassing, and after a moment the Marquis said:

"Finish the sentence, I am interested."

"It sounds rather impertinent . . . and you might be angry."

"I will not be angry, and nothing we say to each other can be impertinence. If we are to work together on our adventure, it is essential for us both to be frank."

"Well . . . I was thinking . . . but I may be wrong that if you carried a . . . lovely lady to bed . . . like the ones Champkins has told me . . . pursue you all the time . . . you would want to do it because it . . . meant something to . . . you."

The Marquis was surprised at what Arina was thinking, but then he realised it was just the way that somebody very young and innocent would think.

"Perhaps you are right," he said casually, "but what I do remember about putting you to bed is that you are far too light for your height, and if you want to please me, you will eat to fill out the hollows in your cheeks and those which I suspect exist elsewhere in your body."

"I will try . . . I promise I will . . . try," Arina said quite naturally, "and already I feel . . . fatter than I was yesterday."

"That is just your imagination," the Marquis replied. "You have a long way to go yet, and that is why I insist that you have a second helping of pigeon or, if you prefer, the veal, although it has not been cooked as well as I would have wished."

"Please . . . I could not eat any more," Arina pleaded. "I will try to be more . . . amenable tomorrow, but I am used to having just an egg for dinner or making some soup for Mama from the vegetables in the garden, or what was left over, and there was usually very little, from what we had for luncheon."

The way she spoke made the Marquis aware that she was not wishing to sound pathetic but was merely telling him the facts of her past life so that he would understand.

"From all I can remember of my father's Castle," he said, "there was certainly plenty of food, and good food, but not cooked as richly as I have come to prefer."

Thinking back into the past, he went on:

"There is salmon in the river and I hope to catch many of them myself, and lobsters from the sea. There is venison from the moors, and when they have grown larger than they are at the moment, lots of grouse and black cock."

"It sounds very exciting!" Arina exclaimed. "And Champkins says there will be haggis."

"Of course," the Marquis agreed. "Haggis and oatmeal for breakfast. That will fatten you up if nothing else does!"

As he spoke he remembered how there had always been a huge bowl of porridge for breakfast in the great Dining-Hall on the First Floor of the Castle.

He remembered filling his wooden bowl edged with silver, which he had been given when he was christened, and adding salt to it. Then, because his father insisted, he walked round the room while he ate it.

It was a tradition of the ancient Scots that they ate their porridge standing, in case while they were doing so they were attacked by a rival Clan.

The Marquis debated whether he would explain this custom to Arina, then realised it was immaterial because the ladies were allowed to eat their porridge sitting, and therefore it would not concern her.

Aloud he said:

"I wonder how many traditions known to my father and other relatives I have forgotten. If I now show my ignorance, it will not only scandalise them but will give them a weapon to use against me."

There was a little silence. Then Arina said:

"I believe it is a . . . mistake for you to . . . think like that."

The Marquis looked at her sharply.

"What do you mean?"

"You said I was to . . . speak the truth . . . and I think you should not return to your home feeling so . . . hostile. Papa always said . . . you get what you give . . . and I think that is . . . true."

The Marquis did not speak, and she went on:

"We are pretending to be married, and I think it would be . . . wise for you to pretend also to be . . . pleased to see your father again . . . pleased to be home. If they are expecting you to be cross and resentful, it will take them by surprise."

As she finished speaking she looked at the Marquis's expression and said quickly:

"I am sorry . . . but you did tell me I could say . . ."

Her eyes were wide and frightened as her words faded away.

Just for a moment the Marquis felt like telling her it was none of her business and she had no right to preach to him. Then as he realised that what she had said was sensible and what he should have thought out for himself, he said:

"I want you always to tell me what is in your mind, Arina, and I am only surprised that you should have thought it all out so sensibly."

"You . . . you are not . . . angry?"

"No, of course not! You only make me feel I have been rather stupid."

"You could . . . never be . . . that!"

"I hope you are right, but you have certainly put things into a different perspective from the way I have been thinking so far."

"I know it is difficult for you, very, very difficult," Arina said in a soft voice, "to leave behind in the South everything that . . . matters to . . . you."

She gave a little sigh, as if she was feeling the same. Then she added quickly:

"I feel as if I am being clairvoyant when I tell you that things will not be so bad as you anticipate."

"How do you know that?"

"I cannot explain it, but I think it is because you are so vital, so vibrant, that any opposition which you think you will encounter will disperse when you are there almost as if you were the sun driving away the mist."

She spoke in a dreamy voice which surprised the Marquis and after a moment he said:

"I hope you are right. Anyway, if the mist is there, as I am afraid it may be, I am sure we can disperse it together."

He saw a light come into her eyes at the word "together," and he knew she was thinking that if she could help him it would be very wonderful for her to be able to do so.

He raised his glass.

"To us, Arina!" he said. "Together on a very strange and, I hope, exciting adventure."

Chapter Six

"It is wonderful! Beautiful! Just the sort of Castle you should have!"

Arina spoke with such a note of exaltation and excitement in her voice that the Marquis felt himself respond in the same way.

He could not help feeling elated from the moment they had arrived in Aberdeen and transferred from the *Sea Serpent* to the Duke's yacht.

When they arrived he thought that quite unexpectedly he had enjoyed the voyage.

He had anticipated that it would be three days and nights of utter boredom. Instead, he found himself enjoying his conversations with Arina, which often became lectures.

At the same time, he found that she not only asked him extremely intelligent questions but was also prepared to argue with him.

When he questioned her as to how she could have such an astute and at times amazingly logical mind, she answered:

"Papa or Mama used to read aloud every evening, and afterwards Mama and I would start an argument with Papa as to whether the writer had been right or wrong in his assumptions. Usually Papa won the contest, but at the same time it was very exciting and we often became quite aggressive!"

She laughed and added:

"That is something I would not . . . dare to do with you."

Nevertheless, the Marquis found that he had to polish up his brain, and when they reached Aberdeen he had to admit that he had been stimulated and amused instead of being depressed by the voyage.

He would have been less than human if he had not found it gratifying to be greeted by a number of the Clan, all looking magnificent in their kilts, who escorted him and Arina to where the Duke's yacht was waiting beside the Quay.

A Piper played them aboard with "Victory to the McDonons," and when the vessel started to move out to sea they were cheered by a crowd that had accumulated to watch and listen.

If Arina was thrilled at her first sight of the Castle, the Marquis felt a sensation of pride that he had never felt before.

There was no Castle on the whole coast of Scotland that looked as magnificent and enchanting as Kildonon.

Situated high above the bay, with only the gardens between it and the sea, it was silhouetted against the moors which rose high against the sky.

It was not only the Castle itself with its turrets and its spires that was so beautiful, but the Marquis had forgotten how the light in that part of Scotland was lovelier than anywhere else in the world.

It seemed to change every few seconds with the movement of the clouds and the sun, and in the centre of the picture the Castle glowed like a precious jewel.

As the yacht sailed across the smooth water they could see a big company of Clansmen waiting for them on the shore, and as the yacht came alongside the long wooden jetty which was built out into the bay, the swirl of the pipes seemed to fill the air.

The Marquis would never have admitted it, but he

found himself wishing at that moment that he were wearing Highland dress, something he had thrown away disdainfully after he had gone South with his mother.

The way he was greeted by the McDonons, the respect with which they approached him, made him once again feel very proud.

As he and Arina were escorted through the gardens to the Castle with two Pipers ahead of them and two following, the Marquis knew he had not only come home but had been accepted as the future Chieftain.

There were flowers in the garden, trees in blossom, and a fountain playing in the centre which threw its water iridescent towards the sun.

There was a great flight of stone steps leading to the balconied terrace, and from there they walked to the front of the Castle so that they could enter by the great wooden iron-studded front door, which had been the entrance since mediaeval times.

Here were more Clansmen, those who were directly connected with the household, and they greeted the Marquis, welcoming him both in English and in Gaelic.

But more eloquent than words were the smiles on their faces and the expressions in their eyes, which proclaimed that they were really pleased to see him.

There was a wide staircase to carry them up to the First Floor, where, as the Marquis knew, there was the Chieftain's Room, in which he was sure his father would be waiting.

There was a wry twist to his lips as he realised that his father was determined from the moment of his arrival to make him aware of his new position and to receive him formally as the prodigal son.

The Major-Domo of the household announced him in stentorian tones:

"The Marquis of Kildonon, Your Grace!"

The Chieftain's Room was so impressive, with the walls hung with the shields and claymores of the past, interspersed with huge portraits of previous Chieftains, that for a moment Arina found it hard to concentrate on the man who was waiting for them.

The Duke was sitting in a high chair that might almost have been a throne at the far end of the room.

She suddenly felt nervous and a little shy as she and the Marquis walked between lines of kilted men standing stiffly at attention.

She was aware too that like those who had greeted the Marquis on the yacht and on the jetty, they regarded her with curiosity.

So far the Marquis had not announced who she was but had merely introduced the Clansmen to her without saying her name.

Now she felt her heart beating quickly, and the only consolation was that she knew she was looking her best.

It was Champkins who had suggested that she wear a gown of deep blue that echoed the colour of the sea, and a bonnet, its pointed brim edged with lace, its crown wreathed with very small pink roses.

The Marquis had looked at her approvingly when she came from her cabin just before they reached Aberdeen.

He had also been aware that it was not only her gown that became her, but that the food she had eaten in the three days they had been at sea had already taken the starved look from her face, the contours of which were already a little fuller.

Now as she moved beside the Marquis she felt that the distance they had to walk in order to reach the Duke seemed interminable.

At last they stopped in front of an old man wearing a huge Cairngorm brooch on his plaid and a large sporran with a top of shining silver on it.

For a moment nobody spoke. Then the Duke, staring at his son from under beetling eye-brows, said in a deep, authoritative voice:

"Welcome home, Alistair. It is good to see you."

He held out his hand and the Marquis grasped it. Then, despite his resolution to do nothing of the sort, in a swift movement his knee touched the ground.

He knew this was an obeisance that his father as Chieftain of the Clan would expect from him, and he had told himself when he thought about it on the voyage that he would be damned if he would humiliate himself. But now it seemed to come naturally to him.

Still with his hand in his father's, he asked:

"How are you, Sir? It has been a long time since we met."

"Too long!" the Duke replied briefly.

Then his eyes, piercing like those of an eagle, turned to stare at Arina.

She knew without his putting it into words what the Duke was asking, and she held her breath because she was frightened.

The Marquis's voice, however, seemed to ring out so that everybody in the room could hear it.

"And now, Father," he said, "may I present to you my wife, who has accompanied me on my voyage here."

"Your wife!"

There was no doubt that the Duke was astonished, but before the Marquis could say any more, he asked sharply:

"You are married? Why did nobody tell me of this?"

"We were married very quietly," the Marquis replied, "for reasons which I will explain to you later."

There was a silence, as if even the Duke found it difficult to know what to say.

Then from the side of the room where she had stood unnoticed came a woman.

With her head held high, she walked to the Duke's side and stood beside his chair, her eyes on the Marquis's face.

She was tall, and handsome in a somewhat masculine manner, with clear-cut features and brown hair with reddish lights in it arranged carelessly under a tartan bonnet which carried on one side of it a brooch which the Marquis recognised as the crest of the McNairns.

There was really no need for the Duke to mumble in a very different tone from what he had used before:

"Lady Moraig, you have not met my son Alistair."

"No, but I have been looking forward to it," Lady Moraig said in a clear, unhesitating voice.

She held out her hand, and as the Marquis took it in his, he said a little mockingly:

"It is certainly a new experience to see a McNairn in this room!"

"My brother and I thought it was time that we buried those foolish feuds which have kept us busy killing one another for hundreds of years."

"I agree with you," the Marquis replied. "Let me present my wife."

The nod Arina received from Lady Moraig made it very obvious that she was an intruder, and she knew that the Duke was already hostile because she was English.

He had obviously never for one moment envisaged that the Marquis would marry somebody so alien to the Clan and to the great majority of Scots.

But, as if he felt that this was neither the time nor the place for recrimination, the Duke rose slowly and stiffly to his feet.

"There are many of our kinsmen here who wish to meet you, Alistair."

The Marquis nodded his agreement, and the Duke moved forward a few paces with his son beside him, and all those in the room filed slowly along to be introduced and to welcome the Marquis home.

Some shook hands, some merely bowed respectfully, but the Marquis managed to have a friendly word with each man, and indeed there were many whom he remembered from the past.

While this was happening, somebody had fetched a chair for Arina and she sat down, but while another was offered to Lady Moraig, she refused it disdainfully.

Instead, she stood stiff and unsmiling a little distance from Arina, making it very obvious that she had no wish to consort with her.

When the introductions were over, the Duke made a

movement as if to leave the Chieftain's Room, and the Marquis looked back and beckoned to Arina.

She jumped up hastily to join him, and as she did so Lady Moraig also approached him.

"What does it feel like to return to the fold after being away for so long?" she asked.

"I will reserve my reply for a little later," the Marquis answered evasively.

The Duke was ahead of them, and as if she refused to acknowledge that Arina was there, Lady Moraig said:

"You know that your father had a plan to unite our Clans in friendship and harmony."

"I understood that you had agreed to marry my brother!"

"Poor Ian," Lady Moraig said in a slightly softer tone, "but we must, you and I, think not only of ourselves but of our people."

"Of course," the Marquis agreed, "and I am looking forward to introducing my wife to the McNairns."

His reply swept the smile from Lady Moraig's lips, and her eyes were hard as she glanced for a moment at Arina.

Then as they reached the door, instead of following the Duke, who was leading the way to the Drawing-Room, she walked down the stairs, and Arina could feel her vibrations of anger and frustration almost as if she expressed them in words of violence.

Impulsively she said in a low voice that only the Marquis could hear:

"I am . . . sorry for . . . her."

"I am grateful to you."

Her eyes met his and she knew that although Lady Moraig was not unattractive in her way, she did not compare favourably with the beautiful ladies whom Champkins had described to her as being infatuated with the Marquis.

She thought of the powder-puff by the mirror on his dressing-table, and thought to herself:

'I am sure he loved only really feminine women, which is something Lady Moraig is not.'

There was no chance of having another intimate word

with the Marquis before they were in the Drawing-Room, where they were joined by the Duke's close relations.

There were a number of male cousins, and elderly and middle-aged women who Arina learnt lived nearby.

There were also one or two teenagers who stared at the Marquis wide-eyed, the boys appreciating the elegance of his fashionable clothes, the girls obviously thinking him extremely handsome.

The conversation was somewhat stilted and constrained until finally the Duke said in a somewhat ominous voice:

"I want to talk to you alone, Alistair. You had better come into the Library."

"Very well, Father," the Marquis replied, "but first I will take Arina to her bedroom so that she can rest before dinner."

"I imagine you know where you are sleeping," the Duke replied briefly.

"Of course," the Marquis agreed.

When they were in the long passage outside the Drawing-Room, Arina gave a little sigh of relief.

The last hour in the Drawing-Room, when she had been doing her best to circumvent the very curious questions of the female relatives, had been a trial that had exhausted her.

Now, however, the Marquis opened a door in the passage and they walked into a large, attractive room with a big carved four-poster bed and an open fireplace big enough to burn logs.

Arina looked round with interest.

The windows overlooked the garden and the sea beyond, and on the carpet were fur rugs made from the skins of wildcats.

It was an austere room and yet it had a majestic air about it.

The Marquis closed the door. Then he said:

"I must congratulate you. You came through what must have been a very trying ordeal with flying colours."

"You really mean that?" Arina asked. "I was so afraid of failing you."

"You saved me!"

"I am well aware that you would not wish to . . . marry Lady Moraig," Arina said in a small voice. "At the same time . . . I think your father . . . hates me!"

"Nevertheless, he believes you to be my wife, and there is nothing he can do about it."

"Lady Moraig was also very . . . angry," Arina went on. "Does this mean that the feud between the Clans will be intensified and you may start . . . fighting all over again?"

She sounded so upset at the prospect that the Marquis laughed.

"Of course not," he said. "We are much more civilised now than we were in the past, and I am quite certain that the elders of both Clans will in time come to respect one another and behave like human beings rather than barbarians!"

"Perhaps it would have been better for . . . everybody if you had . . . married her."

"I would rather die!" the Marquis said sharply. "Or, what would actually have happened—starve!"

He spoke so positively that Arina looked at him, and realising that he was sincere, she said:

"We must be very, very . . . careful not to be found out."

"We will be," the Marquis replied. "Now rest, and be prepared for a very formal dinner. My father dines in state."

As he spoke he went from the room, and as if they had been waiting for him to leave two maids came hurrying in to assist Arina to undress.

*   *   *

As the Marquis came walking back from the river, taking a short-cut towards the Castle, through the heather which was not yet in bud, he thought triumphantly that he had a great deal to boast about.

He had caught no less than four salmon since he had started fishing this morning, and he was delighted to find that he had not lost his skill even though he had not held a fishing-rod in his hand since he was twelve.

Two gillies, laden with the salmon and his rod and gaff, were walking behind him, and he moved quickly ahead of them, eager to get back to boast to Arina of how clever he had been.

'Tomorrow she must come with me,' he decided, and I will teach her how to fish. I am sure it is something she will enjoy.'

It was extraordinary, he thought, how Arina had managed to assimilate herself into the life of the Castle in a manner to which nobody could make any objection, not even the Duke, and apparently she was as pleased with Scotland as he was.

He thought now as he walked towards the Castle that whether he wished to admit it or not, it was his home.

Although he had never expected it and in fact had anticipated that he would hate very moment of being back, he had without effort taken up his life where it had left off fifteen years ago.

He had only to hear the Pipers waking him in the morning as they paraded up and down to feel that the years when he had been in the South were fading away like the mist on the moors.

Whatever his brain might say, he was once again a Scot, living on his own land, with his blood quickening to everything that was traditional.

The pipes, the moors, the mist, and the Clansmen greeting him were all so familiar that he could feel his whole being going out to them.

"I came expecting to hate Scotland, and I love it!" the Marquis had admitted to himself last night.

When he slept in the narrow bed in the Dressing-Room which adjoined Arina's he found himself almost ridiculously resenting the fact that he was not sleeping in the great four-poster which for generations had been the bed of the Chieftain's eldest son.

But the greatest change was in his father.

At first on his arrival he had been astonished, for the Duke seemed to have shrunk and become smaller than he remembered.

Then he knew that what had really happened was that he had grown up and he was no longer frightened of his father as he had been when he was a small boy.

What was more, the Duke was now an old man, and although he was still demanding and authoritative, he was quiet and pleasant unless his authority was opposed in any way.

The Marquis had been prepared to fight him, only to find that there was no necessity for it.

"It is a great disappointment to me, Alistair," the Duke had complained, "that you have married a woman from the South, when I planned for you to take your brother's place and marry Moraig McNain."

"So Faulkner told me," the Marquis replied, "but as I am already married, such an idea is impossible."

"Of course," the Duke agreed, "but it is a pity—a great pity!"

To the Marquis's astonishment, he had left it at that, and although it was obvious that he eyed Arina warily, as if she were not trustworthy, he was not rude to her and she took her rightful place in the house.

"Everything has turned out so much better than I had expected," the Marquis told himself.

As a brace of grouse rose almost at his feet and flew away clucking, he began to look forward to the shooting which would begin in August, and he knew that the Keepers' prophecies were for big bags after good hatching.

He had expected to bewail how he was missing Ascot, his friends at White's Club, and the Balls which would be occurring every night in London.

Instead, it all seemed very far away, as if he were living on another planet.

When he rose in the morning he barely gave them a thought, but was intent on thinking of the people he would be meeting and how soon he could get to the river and start fishing.

He also found himself making plans of how he would alter the way things were done, once he was in the position of authority.

He realised that as his father was growing old, the people under him, while loyal and devoted, had grown lax and needed leadership to keep them up to the mark.

"There is a lot that needs to be done here, Champkins," he said as he was dressing.

"I've noticed that, M'Lord," Champkins replied, "but Your Lordship'll sort it all out, as Your Lordship always does."

The Marquis smiled.

Then this morning when he was leaving for the river he said to Champkins:

"You will find my brothers' clothes somewhere in the Castle. I am sure I am about the same size as Lord Colin. Find me his evening-dress, and I might wear the kilt to go fishing tomorrow."

He left the room and did not see Champkins smile, although he would not have been surprised if he had heard him mutter beneath his breath:

"Can't get away from their own blood. It always gets 'em in the end."

Arina, who had been exploring the garden on her own, realised that the shadows were growing longer, and she was sure the Marquis would soon be returning from fishing and would expect her to pour out his tea.

She hurried up the stone steps, thinking that, as she had thought when she had first seen it, the Castle was enchanted.

Everything about it was so beautiful, so exactly what a Castle should be, and she had run out of words to describe it to her mother.

Inside, when she reached the big marble Hall with its dark oak panelling hung with flags captured by the McDonons in battle, she ran up the stairs, hoping there

would not be too many people for tea so that she could
have the Marquis to herself.

She had learnt that the Castle was always open to any of
their relatives or friends, and they would arrive at any
hour of the day or night, always to be hospitably welcomed.

She went into a smaller Sitting-Room where tea was
arranged on a big round table.

There was nobody there, although as Arina expected
the table was loaded with baps, scones, griddle-cakes,
shortbread, and ginger-biscuits, besides oatcakes, honey
in the comb, and a huge pat of golden butter stamped
with the McDonon crest.

She had grown used to the insignia being on anything
and everything.

She heard a step behind her and turned to see the
Marquis.

She was aware that the sunshine as well as the sea had
already tanned his face, and she thought he looked even
more handsome than he had in London.

"I was looking for you, Arina," he said. "What do you
think? I caught four salmon, one of them over thirteen
pounds!"

He spoke in the triumphant tone of a small boy.

"How splendid!" Arina exclaimed. "I am so glad. Can I
see them?"

"They will be laid out on marble slabs in the larder
downstairs," he answered. "I will show them to you after
tea or tomorrow."

"You must be hungry."

She sat down automatically in front of the silver tray on
which were a kettle, a tea-pot, and all the other parapher-
nalia of tea-making, the silver engraved with the McDonon
crest.

The Marquis started to spread a griddle-cake thickly
with butter, telling her as he did so how he had caught his
fish, lost two others, and been broken by one after he had
played it for fifteen minutes.

He sounded so enthusiastic about it all that as Arina
listened to him she thought it was very different from the

rather bored, supercilious manner in which he had talked when they were in London.

Nobody else arrived for tea, and they went on talking for a long time until the Marquis said:

"I had better go have a bath. I believe there are some people coming over for dinner tonight, but I cannot remember who they are."

"There seems to be a party every evening."

"Why not?" the Marquis asked. "There are plenty of servants to wait on them, and the food is good."

"Too good!" Arina laughed. "I am afraid my new gowns are getting very tight round the waist."

"That is what I want to hear," the Marquis said, "and shall I tell you that you look so much better, and it makes you very lovely."

It was a compliment Arina had not expected, and as the colour rose in her face, she looked away from him because she was shy.

"Very lovely!" the Marquis said again.

Then as Arina raised her eyes to his, it was somehow impossible for either of them to look away.

As the Marquis went to his room to change for dinner and Arina went to hers, she could hear him moving about next door and talking to Champkins, and she wished she could join in and be with the Marquis for a little while longer before people arrived for dinner.

She rang for a maid and changed quickly into a beautiful gown which was embroidered and trimmed with lace.

It was a more elaborate one than those which she usually wore, and she hoped that the Marquis would think it attractive.

As she thought of him she realised that it was quiet in the Dressing-Room, and she thought he was either taking a long time over his bath or else he was already dressed and had gone to the Drawing-Room, where they were to meet before dinner.

Because she was eager to see him, she hurried down the passage, only to find disappointingly that the Drawing-Room was empty.

Then she realised there was still half-an-hour before dinner, and she wondered whether the Marquis had gone out onto the terrace on the floor below.

She went downstairs to the stone terrace, but found again disappointingly that there was nobody there.

The sun was sinking behind the moors, its light dazzling and the sea a very deep blue.

Slowly, feeling once again enchanted by the beauty of it all, Arina walked down the stone steps into the garden.

Here the shadows had grown very much longer, the scent of the roses and stocks seemed to have intensified, and the shrubs were bright with blossoms which also scented the air.

She was just about to move towards the lawn when from the shrubs she heard a curious little whine.

She stood listening, and as the curious little whine came again and again, she wondered if it was an animal caught in a trap.

Because she could not bear to think of it suffering, she pushed aside the shrubs to seek for it, and as she did so she felt something hard strike her on the back of the head.

She gave a little cry of pain before there was darkness and she knew no more. . . .

* * *

Arina slowly came back to consciousness, aware that her head hurt and it was hard to breathe.

Then she knew there was something thick over her face and she was lying on her back.

Because she was so bemused and for the moment only half-conscious, she made no movement.

Then she heard a man's voice say:

"Oi hopes ye did na bruise her. Her Ladyship said there were ta be na marks on her."

"Oi hit her where Oi were told, on th' back o' th' head," another man replied. "Ye'll see na bruising beneath th' hair

Arina was puzzled by the voices.

Then as she was able to think more clearly, she was aware that these must be the men who had struck her down, and her intelligence told her that if she moved they might hit her again.

Vaguely, far away in the back of her mind, she recalled her father telling her how after a battle the soldiers who were wounded pretended to be dead when the scavengers came around to steal everything they possessed.

"If a wounded man tries to prevent them from taking his belongings, they kill him!" her father had said. "On one occasion, it was only by playing dead for several hours that I was able to remain alive."

Her mother had given a cry of horror, but now Arina remembered and lay very still.

At the same time, she tried frantically to understand what was happening to her, and she knew that because the men had mentioned "Her Ladyship," her kidnapping must have been on the instigation of Lady Moraig.

But if they were to kidnap her, why did they have to be so brutal?

She could still feel the aching pain at the back of her head, but she was aware that it might in fact have been worse.

Because she had wanted to look her best for the Marquis she had arranged her hair in quite an elaborate *chignon*, and the maid had secured it with hair-pins and also put on the top of it a little rosette of lace to match her gown.

It had looked very pretty, but now Arina knew that if the blow from the club, or whatever it was that had hit her, had not been cushioned by the thickness of her hair, she would not have regained consciousness so quickly.

"How far have we ta take her?" one of the men asked.

"A bit farther," the other replied, "but not too far. She was supposed ta have rowed herself out ta sea."

"That would na seem likely ta me," the other man replied, "considering she's only a wee bit o' a lassie."

"Because Her Ladyship's so good wi' an oar, she expects other women ta be th' same."

The two men laughed somewhat jeeringly, as if they did not appreciate the more Herculean feats of their Mistress.

"She's a pretty wee creature," one of the men remarked.

"A Sassenach!"

"A wooman's a wooman for a' that!" came the answer.

"That's ye're opinion, Jock, but then ye've always been one wi' th' lassies."

The two men talked in a way which told Arina that they were of a rather better class and perhaps were better educated than if they had been the ordinary rough type of Clansmen.

She was sure that if they were carrying out Lady Moraig's instruction to kidnap her and leave her in a boat out at sea, she would have chosen her most intelligent servants for the job.

Then what she had heard made her aware of exactly what was intended.

The Marquis's two brothers had died at sea when they were out fishing, and now it would appear that she also had rowed herself out from the shelter of the bay and had drowned because she had not the strength to row herself back to shore.

'I suppose they will leave me to drift endlessly on the tide,' she thought, then had a different idea of what the men intended to do.

There was only one man rowing, and the splash of the oars seemed to grow slower and slower until finally he stopped rowing, and his accomplice asked:

"D'ye think this is far enough?"

"Oi reckon so, an' there's a nice bit o' wind gettin' up. 'Twill be rough in a short while."

"Naw, wait a wee bit. Supposing she comes round an' struggles?"

"She'll na do that," the other man said, "but if she does, Oi'll gi' her another hit on th' head."

"Ye'll bruise her!"

Arina imagined that the man who had already spoken shrugged his shoulders.

"By th' time her body's washed ashore, they'll na be lookin' for bruises."

With a little gasp Arina suddenly realised what they were about to do. She could almost see it being planned in Lady Moraig's mind.

She had rowed herself from the Castle because it was a calm, pleasant evening, the boat had upset or else the bung had been knocked out of the bottom of it, and she had drowned.

She wondered frantically if after she had been thrown into the water it would be feasible for her to save herself by swimming.

If after leaving her they became aware that she was in fact a strong swimmer, she was afraid that they would return and hit her again, and, rendered unconscious, she would drown.

"What must I do? Oh, Papa, save me as you saved me before!" she prayed silently.

She felt that her father must hear her, and as he had sent the Marquis to save her mother, he would send him now to save her.

But she had the terrifying feeling that the Marquis would not know of her disappearance until it was time for them to go in to dinner, and even then it might be a long time before anybody would suspect that she was in a boat out at sea.

Whenever she had talked to the Marquis about her life in the country, she had told him how she loved riding.

But there had been no reason to explain that unlike most girls of her age, she could swim because there was a large lake near their cottage. From the time she had been very small, she and her father had swum in it whenever the water was warm enough.

Now she was hoping that her evening-gown would not impede the movement of her legs, and what was more important than anything else was to prevent the men from seeing that she could stay alive in the water.

"Let's get on wi' it!" one of the men said suddenly.

"All reet, all reet!" the other replied irritably. "No point in bein' in a hurry."

"Oi want ta be awa' hame," the other said. "Oi want ma dinner, and we've got a lang way ta go."

The way he spoke told Arina that he was not returning along the coast next to the Castle but across the sea to where the mainland jutted out, which she was aware was the land of the McNains.

"First take th' blanket frae her face," ordered the man who was rowing.

Arina stiffened and lay very still.

She felt the thick blanket over her head that had made it hard to breathe being lifted away, and she knew that both the men were staring at her as she lay still at their feet.

"She's still unconscious," one of them said. "Now get into th' other boat, Jock. Then Oi'll chuck the oars overboard an' pull out th' bung."

"She's a pretty wee thing," Jock remarked.

"That's na yer business. Leave the fish ta appreciate her."

Arina was aware that Jock was pulling another boat, which they must have been towing, up to the side of the one they were in.

He climbed into it, and as the man with the oars let them drop into the sea, Arina felt one of them bang against the side of the boat in which she was lying.

Then the oarsman was groping beneath her feet.

He pulled out the bung, and instantly she was aware of the water beginning to seep in.

Then Jock must have assisted him into the other boat.

"Now get us hame," he said roughly, "an' hurry up aboot it. Oi want ma dinner. Let's get on wi' it!"

Arina had the feeling that he might be having a last glance at her, and only when the sound of the four oars in the water moved away and there was silence except for the lap of the waves did she open her eyes.

The water was rising very quickly and now the boat was half-full, but still she did not move, feeling it cold and wet against her body.

When she knew it would soon cover her face, she first raised her head, then cautiously sat up, feeling as if she were in a bath of cold water.

She looked in the direction of the other boat, and seeing that it was now only a pin-point in the distance, she doubted if the men could see her.

Then she looked back towards the Castle, in the direction from which they had come.

With a sinking of her heart she realised that it was much farther away than she had anticipated, and she had been carried out from the shelter of the bay into the open sea.

Nevertheless, she knew it was possible for her to swim to shore if she took it steadily and did not become exhausted or frozen from the cold water.

'Perhaps I will die,' she thought, 'and that would be terrible for Mama.'

She knew it would also upset the Marquis if she drowned, because that would put him under pressure to marry for the Clan's sake, and she was also certain that Lady Moraig wanted him as a man.

'Of course she loves him because he is so handsome,' Arina thought, 'but she is bad and wicked to have attempted to . . . murder me . . . and the Marquis would be unhappy with . . . her.'

Then she knew, and found it incredible and quite extraordinary at such a moment, that she loved the Marquis.

He had saved her mother and now she must save him.

It was not only because she could not bear to think of him being married to a woman like Lady Moraig, who was not good enough for him in any way, but also because she wanted to be with him as long as he wanted her.

'I love . . . him! I . . . love him!' she thought.

If she died now, her love would be pointless, because she would have failed to help him as she had promised him she would

She looked again at the shore and it seemed even farther away than it had a moment before.

She knew this was because the sun had sunk, dusk was falling, and without the light from the moors, the Castle seemed shrouded in mist.

"Help me, Papa, help me!" Arina prayed.

As the water came a little higher in the boat, she climbed out into the sea.

Chapter Seven

The water was very cold, and as Arina swam and swam she began to feel as if it were impossible to move her legs anymore or bring her hands back to her breast.

She sank lower in the water and felt the sea splash over her mouth and nose.

"I . . . I cannot do . . . it!" she cried. "I . . . can go no farther!"

She tried to see how far it was to the shore, but either her eyes were too weak or it was too dark. As she shut them again she felt that she had miles farther to go before she reached safety, and it was too far.

Then, almost as if she heard her father's voice speaking, she heard the words ring in her ears:

"If you die, the Marquis will have to marry Lady Moraig, and he too will be destroyed!"

Slowly the idea became instilled in her mind, and it was now not only because Lady Moraig would be unattractive to him but also because she was a murderess, and if she murdered once, she could murder again.

"I must . . . save him . . . I must!" Arina told herself.

Again her head was too low in the water and it swelled over her so that she could not breathe.

She felt as if her legs were weighted down with bricks,

and her arms were so tired that she could not thrust them forward.

"I love . . . you!" she cried to the Marquis. "But . . . I can no longer . . . help you!"

Then even as she felt herself sinking, her knees grated against something hard and at the same time her head fell forward and her faced was buried in sand and sea, and she lapsed into unconsciousness.

Then roughly a voice woke her and she felt herself pulled forward.

Somebody was shouting, a man's voice. She could not understand what he said, but he was shouting and dragging her at the same time, and she thought perhaps Lady Moraig's men were going to try to kill her again.

Then she was turned over on her back and she thought that she must be dying and this was the end.

She felt herself drifting away again into an impenetrable darkness, only to be brought back to life when somebody put an arm under her shoulders and lifted her head.

Even as she was touched she knew who it was, and her heart leapt.

"Arina! Arina!"

She heard him calling her, and because she loved him she turned her face against his shoulder. He was there, he was holding her close, and she was safe!

*   *   *

"Another sip, M'Lady," a voice said in a determined tone.

"No . . . no," Arina said weakly. "It is . . . horrible!"

"It'll warm ye, M'Lady. Ye were cold as an icicle when they brought ye in."

She was not cold now, Arina thought, with a hot-water-bottle at her feet and another at her side. Although they were made of stone, she could feel the warmth seeping through her body, just as the neat whisky someone had made her drink was burning its way down her throat and into her chest.

It was hard to open her eyes, but she managed it, and now she could see the carved wooden canopy of the bed overhead, and on the other side of the room a fire was burning in the big open grate.

She knew where she was, she was alive, she had saved the Marquis, and there was no need to go on fighting anymore.

It had been a long, long swim, but she had managed it.

She shut her eyes again, and as she did so, she heard the Housekeeper say:

"Her Ladyship's asleep, M'Lord, but she's all right. Gawd must have saved her."

"I think she saved herself," the Marquis answered quietly.

Arina wanted to tell him that she had done it for him, but it was impossible to make the effort, and she drifted away again, warm and safe, into a dreamless sleep.

*   *   *

She woke and knew that she had slept for a long time, for the night was past and now it was day.

The curtains were drawn back and the sunshine was coming through the windows.

She stirred, and instantly the Housekeeper, who had looked after her last night, was beside her.

"Are ye awake, M'Lady?"

Arina nodded but it was difficult to find her voice.

"What Your Ladyship wants is sommat to eat," the Housekeeper said briskly, "and ye've had a real good night's rest."

Arina stirred as if she wanted to be certain that her arms and legs, which had felt numb and cold as if they did not belong to her, were still there.

Then as the Housekeeper bustled from the room she lay looking up at the carved canopy on which inevitably was the insignia of the McDonons.

She was thanking God and her father for having brought her to safety.

Then with a little shiver she thought that Lady Moraig

might try again, and she thought perhaps she would be wise to leave soon, so that she would not be a trouble and an encumbrance to the Marquis.

He could still pretend that he was married, but she would not be there to be stalked by Lady Moraig as if she were a wild animal, and hated by the Duke because she was English.

'If I leave . . . perhaps I shall . . . never see him again,' she thought.

Then, because she was so weak and because she loved him, tears ran down her cheeks.

* * *

Later, after Arina had eaten and slept and eaten again, she felt so much better that she no longer wished to stay in bed.

The Marquis had not come to see her and she suspected that he had gone fishing.

Because she wanted to know for certain, when the Housekeeper came to see how she was, she asked:

"Where is the Marquis?"

"He should be hame soon, M'Lady. He went fishin' this morning while ye were still asleep, but I knows His Lordship'll be coming to see ye as soon as he returns."

The Housekeeper left the room and Arina got out of bed to go to the dressing-table and brush her hair. Then she looked at her face in the mirror.

She had expected to look haggard and strained after what had happened yesterday, making her face lined and ugly.

Instead, her eyes seemed very large and bright, her skin very white, and with her hair falling over her shoulders she would have been insincere if she had not known that she looked attractive.

As if reassured by her reflection, she went back to bed, aware that she felt a little shaky on her legs, and waited.

After a while there was a knock on the door, then without waiting for an answer the Marquis came in.

Her eyes lit up at the sight of him, then she gave a little gasp, for it was the first time she had ever seen him wearing the kilt. She thought that even with the plain sporran and ordinary tweed jacket with leather buttons, he looked magnificent.

He walked to the bedside to take her hand in both of his.

"I do not have to ask if you are feeling better," he said in his deep voice. "I can see that you are."

"Much . . . much better. In fact there is no need for me to be so . . . lazy and . . . stay in bed."

"You must take care of yourself."

She had the strange feeling that while their lips were saying one thing, their eyes said something else.

The Marquis seated himself on the mattress facing her and asked:

"Are you well enough to tell me what happened?"

Arina felt shy. She felt it was somehow embarrassing to tell him that the woman had tried to murder her because she wanted him.

Then, as if the Marquis thought it would make things easier, he said:

"I do not believe for a moment that you rowed yourself out to sea."

"It . . . it was . . . two men," Arina answered. "I went . . . into the garden. I was looking . . . for you."

The Marquis's eyes were on her face, but he did not interrupt.

She went on to tell him how she had thought she heard an animal crying in the shrubs, that she had been hit on the back of the head, and that when she had regained consciousness she was lying in the bottom of a boat.

"Your head is all right now?" the Marquis asked quickly.

"There is only a very slight bruise," Arina answered, "because I had arranged my hair with great care so as to look elegant for . . ."

She stopped, knowing that she had been about to say something too revealing.

It was in fact difficult to speak naturally while the Marquis was still holding her hand in his.

Because he was touching her, she could feel a strange feeling like little shafts of sunshine running up her arms and into her breasts.

She knew it was love and thought that just to look at him made her heart beat so violently that she was afraid he would be aware of it.

She could imagine nothing more humiliating than for the Marquis to know that she had fallen in love with him, when in order to save her mother she was playing the role he had asked of her.

'I must be very, very careful,' Arina thought to herself.

Quickly, her words falling over one another, she told the Marquis what she had heard the men saying while she was lying in the boat.

When she repeated the way in which they had spoken of "Her Ladyship," she knew that he stiffened and his fingers tightened on hers.

Without stopping, she described how they had taken away the bung and rowed off, and when the boat had become nearly full of water and was sinking she had started to swim back towards the Castle.

"How could you swim so far?" the Marquis asked.

"I used to swim in a lake with my father when we lived in the country," Arina replied, "but never such a long distance . . . or in a cold sea."

"It was very, very brave of you, and I know of no other woman who would have been so clever and so courageous."

"I . . . I had to save . . . you," Arina said without thinking.

"Me?" the Marquis questioned. "Or yourself?"

"I do not . . . matter," Arina replied, "but I knew that if I . . . died, your father would force you to . . . marry Lady Moraig . . . and it would make . . . you unhappy."

"Would that have worried you?" the Marquis asked softly.

Arina drew in her breath, feeling a little wildly that she wanted his happiness more than anything else in the world.

It was something she could not give him, but she could at least save him from being positively miserable.

She did not answer, and after a moment the Marquis said:

"I want you to tell me, Arina, why you were worried in case I should be unhappy."

"You . . . you have been so . . . kind to me that I want to . . . help you."

"You have helped me already, and when I picked you up off the beach and you turned your head against my shoulder, I felt that you were happy to be with me."

Because his voice was very low and deep, and yet at the same time there was a pleading note in it which she had never heard before, Arina's fingers tightened on his.

"I . . . I thought I was . . . dead," she said in a whisper, "but when you . . . touched me I came . . . alive again."

The Marquis did not answer, and because his silence was rather strange, she looked at him.

Then as their eyes met she felt herself quiver with a feeling she had never known before, which seemed to be rising within her, and making her feel that it was impossible to breathe.

"I may be quite wrong," the Marquis said after a moment, "but I have the feeling, Arina, that you love me."

Because his eyes were holding hers captive, it was impossible not to tell the truth.

"Yes . . . I . . . love you!" Arina whispered. "I love you . . . and I want to . . . help you . . . but I will not be a . . . nuisance, and as . . . soon as you . . . want me to leave, I/ will do so . . . as I promised . . . without making any . . . fuss."

"That will not be for at least a million years," the Marquis answered quietly.

As he spoke he bent forward and his lips were on hers.

For a moment she could not believe it was happening. Then a rapture seemed to invade her whole body, and it was so vivid, so insistent, that it was like a streak of lightning.

She felt as if the Marquis gave her the sunshine that was outside and carried her high over the moors behind them and into the sky.

He slipped his arm round her to hold her close against him while he kissed her, and she felt that after all she had been through, she was in a Heaven that was Divine, and so utterly and completely wonderful that it would be an agony to leave it.

Then she knew that this was what she had always wanted.

It was the love her mother had had for her father and he for her, and nothing else was of any importance except a love that filled the world, the sky, and the sea, and there was nothing else but love.

The Marquis raised his head and said:

"I love you!"

"H-how can you?" Arina asked. "There are so many beautiful women whom you . . . could love."

"The 'beautiful women,' as you call them," he said with a smile, "are all far away and forgotten, and when I saw you lying on the shore and thought you were dead, I knew that what I felt for you was different from anything I have ever felt before."

"You . . . you love me! You really love . . . me?"

"It will take me a long time, as I have said, at least a million years, to tell you how much."

"I . . . I cannot . . . believe it! You are so magnificent, so kind, so . . . wonderful! I thought you were a messenger from God, sent to save Mama, and not a man who would . . . love me."

The Marquis smiled.

"I am a man, and I find you so alluring, so beautiful, and so very, very exciting, my darling, that I cannot believe I am so fortunate as to find now what I have always been seeking."

He pulled her a little closer as he said:

"Just as you told me we were setting out on an adventure like Odysseus and Jason, like them I have found what I sought."

"Was it . . . love?" Arina asked.

"Love!" the Marquis replied firmly. "Real love, and a love which made you see me as a Knight."

"That is what . . . you have always . . . been."

"That is something you will make me in the future, or rather, a good Chieftain to my Clan."

Arina drew in her breath.

"You mean . . . ?"

"I mean that I am going to stay here," the Marquis interrupted, "and live the life to which I belong and look after my people."

His lips were against the softness of her cheek as he said:

"I think you already know that I cannot do that properly without you to help me."

"Are you sure . . . really sure . . . that you . . . want me?"

"Very, very sure."

Arina drew in her breath. Then she said:

"I have something to tell you . . ."

"And I have a lot to tell you," the Marquis interrupted, "but I know that my father is anxious to see you. Do you think you are well enough to come down to dinner? You can go back to bed immediately afterwards."

"Of course I am well enough," Arina said. "I want to be with . . . you."

The Marquis did not answer. He merely kissed her again.

She could feel his heart beating against hers and that she could excite him seemed the most wonderful thing she could ever imagine.

A knock on the door made the Marquis move away from her, and the Housekeeper came in.

"I am glad you are here, Mrs. McDonon," the Marquis said. "Her Ladyship is coming down to dinner, but I promise we will not keep her up too long."

"She's not to get over-tired, Master Alistair."

The Marquis laughed.

"If she does, you will doubtless scold me as you used to

do when I tore my clothes or stole the apples out of your Sitting-Room."

He did not wait for the Housekeeper to reply but went through the communicating door into the Dressing-Room.

"He was always an awful mischievous laddie!" Mrs. McDonon exclaimed.

She talked of the Marquis's escapades when he was young all the time she was helping Arina to dress, and she thought how wonderful it would be if she could ever have a son who, like his father, would be mischievous in the great Castle which was a perfect playground for children.

When she was ready, she realised, because she had been listening to what Mrs. McDonon was saying rather than thinking about herself, that she was wearing a very lovely evening-gown which made her look like a bride.

It was a gown which she had not even seen before, because it had arrived at the last moment just before they left for Tilbury, and she thought perhaps the Marquis might think she was over-dressed.

But when he came through the communicating door she saw by the expression in his eyes and the look on his face what he thought of her.

If she looked smart, so did he, and in his evening-dress with a lace jabot at his neck and the silver buttons on his coat polished until they shone like jewels, he was so magnificent that she felt no man could be so handsome or so overwhelmingly attractive.

His sporran was as elaborate as the one the Duke wore, and the Cairngorm on top of his *skean dhu*, which was worn in his hose, sparkled like a star.

As they walked towards the centre of the Castle the Marquis said:

"I want to tell you how beautiful you are and how much I love you!"

Arina slipped her hand into his.

"I was . . . trying to find words to tell you how handsome you look . . . wearing the kilt."

"It is a good thing that you admire me as much as I

admire you," the Marquis smiled, "Otherwise I should be jealous."

Arina gave a little laugh.

"I hope you . . . will be . . . then you will . . . know what I would be . . . feeling."

It was impossible to say any more, for one of the servants approached the Marquis with some letters on a silver salver.

"The post has just arrived, M'Lord."

The Marquis took the letters without much interest, then as they walked into the Drawing-Room to find it empty he opened one quickly and started to read it.

Arina stood in front of the fireplace, thinking how impressive the room was, and yet so different from any Drawing-Room in the South.

The ceiling was very high, the windows set in stone were diamond-paned, and the walls were hung with portraits of previous Chieftains.

Some of the furniture was French and she knew it dated from the time when Mary Queen of Scots had brought the French influence to Scotland.

The Marquis looked up from his letter.

"I have some good news for you, my darling."

"Good news?"

The Marquis glanced down at the letter in his hand.

"When I told my secretary in London to pay the hundred pounds that was owing to your mother's Surgeon, I told him I wished to know immediately the result of the operation, and that the information must come directly to me in case it was bad news."

"Mama is . . . all right?"

"The operation has been completely successful, and your mother is recovering much quicker than the Surgeon dared to hope!"

Arina clasped her hands together. Then she gave a little cry of sheer happiness and flung herself against the Marquis.

"It is all due to . . . you! If you had not given us the money, Mama would have . . . died."

Her voice broke on the words, and there were tears in her eyes, but they were tears of happiness.

The Marquis held her very close against him.

"I am so glad, so very glad, my darling."

"I am sure it was Papa who sent . . . you to us, and now Mama can get . . . well, and perhaps find happiness again."

"We will make her happy," the Marquis promised.

Arina was about to reply when there was a step in the doorway and the Duke came into the Drawing-Room.

Feeling a little embarrassed, she moved away from the Marquis, knowing his father had seen her in his arms.

The Duke joined them at the hearth-rug and Arina curtseyed.

"You are better?" the Duke asked in a more kindly tone than he had used to her before.

"Yes, thank you, Your Grace, much better."

"I understand you were very brave."

He did not wait for Arina to reply but said:

"Outside is the man who found you as you reached the shore. He is an old man, but his eyes were bright enough to see you when you collapsed in the shallow water. You were lying face-down, and if he had not saved you by pulling you up onto dry land, you might have drowned."

Arina gave a little murmur and felt the Marquis's hand touch hers.

"I told Malcolm McDonon to come here so that you could thank him," the Duke said.

"Yes, of course, I would like to do that."

The Duke walked ahead and she and the Marquis followed.

Standing outside the Drawing-Room at the top of the stairs was an old Clansman with a grey beard, nervously twisting his bonnet as he waited for them.

He touched his forehead respectfully as the Duke came up to him.

"I have brought the Marchioness to meet you, Malcolm," the Duke said slowly, "and I have told her it was your quick eyes, which are those of a stalker, that saw her on the beach and saved her life."

The old man murmured something, and the Duke said to Arina:

"He understands if you speak slowly to him, but he himself can speak only the Gaelic."

Arina held out her hand and Malcolm McDonon said in Gaelic:

"I am very glad to have been of service to Your Ladyship."

Arina understood, and without thinking she answered him in his own language:

"*Tapadh Leat Tha Ni Glé Thaiwgeal,*" which meant: "Thank you. I am very grateful."

Only when she had spoken did she see the delight in Malcolm's face and become aware of the astonishment in the Duke's and the Marquis's.

There was a moment's silence, then the Duke gave Malcolm McDonon an envelope which Arina guessed contained money.

He thanked him in Gaelic, and as he walked down the stairs the Duke looked penetratingly at Arina.

"You speak Gaelic?" he asked sharply.

"A . . . little."

"Who taught you?"

She hesitated, then told the truth.

"My mother."

"How can your mother know Gaelic?"

"She . . . she is . . . Scottish."

Arina spoke in a low voice and was obviously embarrassed.

Then the Marquis, as if he could not control his curiosity, enquired:

"Why did you not tell me?"

She looked up at him and answered in a voice he could barely hear:

"I . . . I thought you might be . . . angry."

"Angry? Why should I be angry?"

She did not answer, and after a moment, as if he guessed the answer, he enquired:

"Who is your mother?"

She put out her hands as if she would hold on to him,
then dropped them to her sides.

"My . . . mother," she faltered, "is a . . . McNain."

The Marquis seemed unable to speak, and the Duke
exclaimed:

"A McNain? Why was I not told? Why have you been so
secretive about it?"

As if it was easier to answer him than the Marquis,
Arina replied:

"My mother ran away with my father, and because he
was English, my grandfather, who was the . . . Chieftain
of the McNains, was furious and refused to have anything
. . . more to do with . . . her."

The Duke stared at Arina as if he could hardly believe
what he was hearing. Then he said:

"Come into the Drawing-Room."

As he spoke, Arina knew he was aware that the servants
at the foot of the stairs could hear what they were saying.

The Duke walked ahead, and as Arina followed him
obediently, the Marquis took her hand in his, and she
knew that he was not angry but supporting and loving her.

She held her head up and, speaking clearly and calmly,
gave the Duke the explanation for which he was waiting.

"Although my mother was deeply hurt by her father's
anger and his refusal to have anything more to do with her
because she had married an Englishman, she and Papa
were so happy together that it did not really matter."

"Your grandfather was the Earl of Nain?" the Duke
asked sharply.

"Yes, Your Grace, but after she ran away, Mama never
used her . . . title."

"He was a good Chieftain," the Duke said, "but he
loathed us almost as much as he loathed the English!"

The Marquis laughed.

"That was the attitude of all the McNains, as far back as
I can remember. What are you going to do about Lady
Moraig?"

The Duke's lips tightened.

"She will be dealt with by the elders of her Clan and sent away."

"Can you arrange that?"

"The Chieftain will do so when I tell him what happened, and the men who carried out her orders will be punished."

The Marquis felt his father had more to say, so he waited.

"Lady Moraig is only a half-sister of the present Earl," the Duke explained, "and they have never cared for each other. But as Chieftain he is eager that there should be peace between our people, and that problem is already solved, Alistair, for you have married a McNain. I am sure also that he would welcome home Arina's mother, his sister, if she will return to her family."

"Do you really mean that?" Arina cried. "I know it would make Mama very happy, for after Papa's death I know she often longed for her own family."

"That is what we will give her as soon as she is well enough to travel," the Marquis said quietly.

Because she felt so happy, Arina forgot that the Duke was there and pressed her cheek against his shoulder.

With a note of laughter in his voice he said:

"You see, Father, after all my misdeeds and the years which as far as you were concerned I spent in the wilderness, I have come back doing the right thing and bringing you what you had not expected—exactly the wife you wanted me to marry."

There was no need for words.

The Duke merely put his hand on his son's shoulder with a gesture that was very eloquent.

*   *   *

Although the dinner had been a long one, as there were quite a number of guests, and the Piper who played round the table at the end of the meal had played two extra tunes which Arina knew were to celebrate her escape from death, she was not tired.

However, she had gone to bed immediately dinner was finished, and Mrs. McDonon had helped her to undress and left a candle alight by the big four-poster bed, and there was a log fire burning in the fireplace.

"There's a chill wind coming frae the sea tonight, M'Lady," she said as she looked out. "'Twill be a miracle if ye don't catch cold after all ye've been through."

Arina did not answer but lay back against the pillows, thinking how warm and comfortable she was and so happy that she felt as if little flames from the fire were moving inside her, lighting her whole body.

She was waiting, and it was less than thirty minutes later when the communicating door opened.

The Marquis came into the room, and now he was no longer wearing Highland dress but a long velvet robe which she had never seen before but which she thought became him equally well.

He walked towards the bed and she realised there was a strange light in his eyes that made her feel shy and yet at the same time wildly excited.

She held out her hands towards him.

"I was sure . . . you would come to . . . say good-night," she murmured.

The Marquis sat down as he had earlier in the day, facing her on the mattress.

"Good-night?" he questioned. "I think, darling, you have forgotten something."

She looked puzzled.

"What . . . could I have forgotten . . . except to thank you over and over . . . again?"

"You have thanked me enough already."

"Then what can I have . . . forgotten?"

"That we are married!" the Marquis said in his deep voice.

Arina's eyes dropped before his.

"You said it was only . . . pretence."

"I said that when I was behaving like an Englishman and our contract was English. In Scotland, we have declared ourselves to be man and wife in front of witnesses, and we are legally married by the laws of this country."

Arina felt as if every word he spoke was an exaltation of joy rising up into the sky.

"I have today already written to Edinburgh to register our marriage," he added.

As if she thought it was too wonderful to be true, Arina asked:

"You are . . . sure? Quite sure . . . that is what you want?"

"I am quite sure," the Marquis replied, "and that is what I intend to have! You are mine, Arina, my wife, now and forever, and I will never let you go!"

She thought he would put his arms round her, but instead he waited for a moment. Then he said:

"You know how much I want you, not only with my body but with my mind, my heart, and my soul. But you have been through a terrible experience, and if you wish I will just say good-night to you and leave you to rest."

Arina knew that only a man who was an idealist and the Knight she believed him to be could be so understanding.

Because she could find no words to tell him so, she could only hold out both her arms and pull him towards her. . . .

* * *

A long time later, when the fire was only a golden glow and the flames had died down, the Marquis said:

"I wish there were words in which I could tell you what it means to be here with you in my own home, on my own land, surrounded by the people who love and respect me and whom I will serve as long as I live."

"That is just how I want you to feel," Arina answered.

He drew her closer to him, feeling the softness of her body and knowing that only to touch her was to be aware that he touched the perfection he had always sought in a woman.

"How can I have been so lucky as to have found you?" he asked.

"I am sure you will think it is a . . . strange thing to

say, but it was Papa who guided me when I was so . . . desperate and who sent me first to Lady Beverley and in some magical way arranged that you should overhear my conversation with her."

Arina paused. Then she said:

"Only a man with the real instincts of kindness could have helped me as you did."

"It was not only your father but your prayers, my darling, which told me what to do."

As the Marquis spoke he thought it was a strange thing for him to say and to believe.

Yet, he had known ever since his return to the Castle that the supercilious cynicism that had governed the way he thought and talked with his friends at White's and with the women who came and went in his life had vanished.

But now he thought to himself that it was impossible in Scotland to be anything but honest.

He knew that just as Arina had anticipated that the beauty of the Castle and the moors would lift his mind from everything that was small and petty, they had in fact made him bigger in himself than he had ever been in the past.

Now, for the first time, he could understand his father's air of omnipotence and his desire not only for the greatness of the Clan but also for the greatness of Scotland.

He turned his head to look down at Arina and thought in the light of the dying fire that nobody could look more lovely or more spiritual and that she was different from every other woman he had ever known.

He could see her eyes looking at him adoringly, and he told himself he would never fail her and vowed in the future to live up to her ideals.

A falling log made the flames in the fire leap for a moment and illuminate both the Marquis's face and Arina's, and as they looked at each other instinctively their bodies moved closer.

"I love you!" he said.

"I did not know that love could be so wonderful . . . I feel as if we journeyed together through the stars to a Heaven where there is only . . . love."

The way Arina spoke was very moving, and the Marquis's lips touched her cheek before he asked:

"Is that what I made you feel?"

"That, and so much more. But how can I put into words the . . . ecstasy that is . . . God, and yet is me at the same time?"

"My precious little love!" the Marquis exclaimed.

"I have made . . . you happy?"

"So happy that there are no words for what we feel for each other. It is an ecstasy and at the same time very human, because I can touch you and know that you are mine, not only as a woman but part of my very blood."

"Because I am a Scot."

"As I am, and our children will be, and their children after that."

The Marquis paused before he said:

"How could I ever have imagined that I could escape from Scotland and what it means to those who are born here, in whose blood runs an instinct that raises them from human to the Divine?"

"That is . . . what I . . . feel," Arina said breathlessly.

"We feel the same, and we are the same," the Marquis said. "We are one person, my darling."

She put her arm round his neck to draw him closer still, and as she did so she was aware that just as the flames were flickering over the logs, so flames were flickering in them both.

It was ecstatic and at the same time so intense that it was a pain as well as a pleasure.

"I want you!" the Marquis said.

"I love . . . you!" Arina replied. "Oh, darling, please love me . . . please make me . . . yours . . . so that as you say . . . we are one person."

The Marquis's lips came down on hers and she felt his heart beating against her breast.

Then he was carrying her high over the moors and up into the sky, and as he made her his, they reached a special Heaven where there was only the Divine Love, which is Eternal.

ABOUT THE AUTHOR

BARBARA CARTLAND is the bestselling authoress in the world, according to the *Guinness Book of World Records*. She has sold over 200 million books and has beaten the world record for five years running, last year with 24 and the previous year with 24, 20, and 23.

She is also an historian, playwright, lecturer, political speaker and television personality, and has now written over 320 books.

She has also had many historical works published and has written four autobiographies as well as the biographies of her mother and that of her brother, Ronald Cartland, who was the first Member of Parliament to be killed in the last war. This book has a preface by Sir Winston Churchill and has just been republished with an introduction by Sir Arthur Bryant.

Love at the Helm, a novel written with the help and inspiration of the late Earl Mountbatten of Burma, Uncle of His Royal Highness Prince Philip, is being sold for the Mountbatten Memorial Trust.

In 1978, Miss Cartland sang an Album of Love Songs with the Royal Philharmonic Orchestra.

She is unique in that she was #1 and #2 in the Dalton List of Bestsellers, and one week had four books in the top twenty.

In private life Barbara Cartland, who is a Dame of the Order of St. John of Jerusalem, Chairman of the St. John Council in Hertfordshire and Deputy President of the St. John Ambulance Brigade, has also fought for better conditions and salaries for midwives and nurses.

As President of the Royal College of Midwives (Hertfordshire Branch) she has been invested with the first badge of Office ever given in Great Britain, which was subscribed to by the midwives themselves.

Barbara Cartland is deeply interested in vitamin therapy and is President of the British National Association for Health. Her book, *The Magic of Honey*, has sold throughout the world and is translated into many languages.

She has a magazine "Barbara Cartland's World of Romance" now being published in the USA.

Barbara Cartland

The world's bestselling author of romantic fiction. Her stories are always captivating tales of intrigue, adventure and love.

☐	22611	CAUGHT BY LOVE	$1.95
☐	22513	MUSIC FROM THE HEART	$1.95
☐	20815	MOMENTS OF LOVE	$1.95
☐	20948	LOVE RULES	$1.95
☐	20747	LIES FOR LOVE	$1.95
☐	20746	THE VIBRATIONS OF LOVE	$1.95
☐	20574	LOOKING FOR LOVE	$1.95
☐	20235	LOVE WINS	$1.95
☐	20505	SECRET HARBOUR	$1.95
☐	20234	SHAFT OF SUNLIGHT	$1.95
☐	20014	GIFT OF THE GODS	$1.95
☐	20126	AN INNOCENT IN RUSSIA	$1.95
☐	20013	RIVER OF LOVE	$1.95
☐	14503	THE LIONESS AND THE LILY	$1.75
☐	14133	THE PRUDE AND THE PRODIGAL	$1.75
☐	13032	PRIDE AND THE POOR PRINCESS	$1.75
☐	14360	SIGNPOST TO LOVE	$1.75
☐	14361	FROM HELL TO HEAVEN	$1.75
☐	14902	WINGED MAGIC	$1.95
☐	14922	A PORTRAIT OF LOVE	$1.95